He left the house moments later, climbing into his taxi without so much as a backward glance, let alone a word of thanks or farewell.

And that was that, Lucy thought with a sigh of relief. Put the whole episode down to experience and forget it, she told herself . . .and the man in question. But it wasn't in her nature to give up, whatever difficulties lay in her path, and there was only one person responsible for her sense of failure—Matthew Fenn.

One word of gratitude, even a smile, and she'd have probably been prepared to stick it out for the week at least, but no, the man was clearly devoid of every vestige of human warmth!

WE HOPE you're enjoying our new addition to our Contemporary Romance series—stories which take a light-hearted look at the Zodiac and show that love can be written in the stars!

Every month you can get to know a different combination of star-crossed lovers, with one story that follows the fortunes of a hero and heroine when they embark on the romance of a lifetime with somebody born under another sign of the Zodiac. This month features a sizzling love affair between **Pisces** and **Scorpio**.

To find out more fascinating facts about this month's featured star sign, turn to the back pages of this book...

ABOUT THIS MONTH'S AUTHOR

Helena Dawson, who lives in a Kentish village, says: 'I only launched into a writing career when my sons had flown from the parental nest, and, as an imaginative Gemini, I found romantic fiction an ideal outlet for my creative fantasies.

My hobbies include my dog, gardening, painting and music, but the Mercurial side of my nature is kept in balance by my husband, an Aquarian academic with his feet firmly on the ground, who does not allow me to sidetrack from my work—at least not *very* often, and only when the sun is shining...'

SHADOW ON THE SEA

BY

HELENA DAWSON

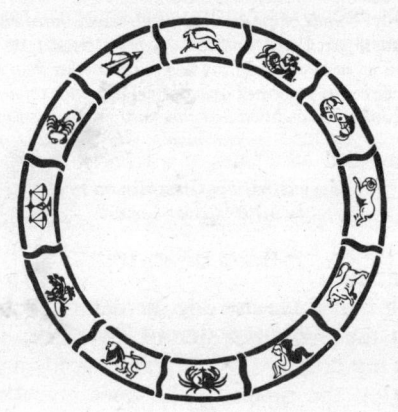

MILLS & BOON LIMITED
ETON HOUSE   18–24 PARADISE ROAD
RICHMOND   SURREY   TW9 1SR

All the characters in this book have no existence outside the imagination of the Author, and have no relation whatsoever to anyone bearing the same name or names. They are not even distantly inspired by any individual known or unknown to the Author, and all the incidents are pure invention.

All Rights Reserved. The text of this publication or any part thereof may not be reproduced or transmitted in any form or by any means, electronic or mechanical, including photocopying, recording, storage in an information retrieval system, or otherwise, without the written permission of the publisher.

This book is sold subject to the condition that it shall not, by way of trade or otherwise, be lent, resold, hired out or otherwise circulated without the prior consent of the publisher in any form of binding or cover other than that in which it is published and without a similar condition including this condition being imposed on the subsequent purchaser.

*First published in Great Britain 1992
by Mills & Boon Limited*

© Helena Dawson 1992

*Australian copyright 1992
Philippine copyright 1992
This edition 1992*

ISBN 0 263 77439 2

STARSIGN ROMANCES is a trademark of Harlequin Enterprises B.V., Fribourg Branch. Mills and Boon is an authorised user.

*Set in 10 on 11 pt Linotron Plantin
01-9202-57627 Z
Typeset in Great Britain by Centracet, Cambridge
Made and printed in Great Britain*

CHAPTER ONE

'SO WHERE'S your elusive fiancé now? And what's so important it's keeping him away on your birthday?'

'Stephen?'

With a little sigh Lucy sat down at the dressing-table and stared bleakly up at her friend, instinctively covering her bare left hand with a protective gesture Bella was quick to intercept.

'Lucy, show me your hand! You're not wearing your ring, are you?' She peered closely at Lucy's face. 'What's happened? You haven't, have you. . .?'

Lucy nodded slowly. 'I've broken off the engagement,' she said bluntly. 'And not very bravely, either,' she added with a rueful half-smile. 'Stephen's away in Munich, setting up a new office or something, and I've written to him there, sending his ring back.'

Her slim shoulders hunched, giving her a waif-like appearance, and Bella crouched down and put an impulsive arm round her friend as Lucy went on, 'It was no use, Bella. All I ever wanted was to love him and marry him and make a home for him, but he'd never come to the point and fix a date for the wedding. And then when——'

She broke off abruptly and sprang to her feet to wander about the bedroom, touching things absently as she passed. 'I don't think, when it comes down to it, he ever really wanted to commit himself to marriage—and a wife. Oh, he was happy enough to make use of me as a hostess, and I was glad to cater for his business dinners and all that, but every time I brought up the subject of our settling down together he'd dismiss it—say he hadn't got time to discuss it. Implying he'd got better things to think about,' she added bitterly.

She swung round to face Bella. 'Then he said he was going abroad again, and he didn't know for how long, and, when I suggested coming out to see him at the end of my last job, he said it would only distract him. . .and there were other things, too. . .'

Lucy's eyes glazed over as her voice trailed away miserably. 'We don't—didn't—seem to have anything in common any more, so I decided to end the whole thing.'

There was a silence while Bella racked her brain for the right thing to say. She'd never liked Stephen le Breton, and she couldn't pretend, not in all honesty, that she was sorry.

'Lucy's far too good for that selfish stick,' Bella had protested to Phil, her husband, when Lucy's engagement had been announced. 'He doesn't deserve a sweet girl like that—you mark my words, he only wants her around for what he can get out of her. He's using her.'

And now she had been proved right, but it gave her no satisfaction to see Lucy so unhappy.

She scrambled to her feet and hugged her friend, feeling the slight body tremble in her arms.

'You've done the right thing, Lou,' she told her quietly. 'You'll see that in time, I know. Stephen wasn't right for you, but it can't have been an easy thing to do, sending his ring back.'

Lucy's head moved against her shoulder in mute assent, and Bella's arms tightened round her.

'Still, try to forget it, if you can, just for this evening at least,' Bella encouraged her. 'Let's go and join the others now——' She broke off with a worried frown. 'Perhaps it wasn't such a good idea fixing this party after all, but——'

'But you weren't to know.' Lucy managed a small

smile. 'And I couldn't not have come, could I, not when you'd gone to all this trouble, and just for my birthday?'

She straightened up and tossed her hair back with a defiant gesture. 'Hang on a minute while I fix my face again. How do I look?'

She peered at her immaculate reflection in the mirror to check her appearance, then stood up, squaring her shoulders.

'You look fine,' Bella assured her, 'and that's a stunning dress. Dark blue really suits you. Is it new?'

Lucy pulled a face. 'It cost the earth, actually, but I couldn't resist it. It's my birthday present to myself.'

She stopped to put her hand impulsively on Bella's arm. 'It's really sweet of you and Phil to throw this party, Bella. I must confess I was feeling a bit low after my last job—apart from anything else,' she added not quite steadily, 'they were such lovely people, the Corrigans, and my flat felt pretty lonely after that huge house full of people all the time. Then you rang. . . That's when I went and got this dress.'

She gave a twirl at the top of the stairs, making the silky material flow out round her like waves.

Bella laughed. 'We didn't like the thought of your being all alone, and you know Phil—always looking for an excuse for a party!'

She led the way downstairs, adding, 'It's nothing very grand, you know. Only a buffet—which is a good thing as it's turned out, as I wasn't sure till the last minute how many there would be. Phil had the idea he ought to ask a business colleague who's had a rough time recently, but at the last minute he cried off. He's still recovering from a bad skiing accident, apparently, and decided he wasn't up to socialising just yet.'

'Anyone I know?' Lucy asked interestedly.

'Shouldn't think so. A man called Matthew Fenn. I

haven't actually met him myself. As I said, it was Phil's idea to invite him.'

'Matthew Fenn?' Lucy repeated slowly with a note in her voice that made Bella turn to look at her.

'Why, do you know him?'

Lucy frowned. 'I don't know. The name rings a bell, somehow, but I can't put a face to it. Maybe I've met him at someone's house—I do get around, you know!'

Bella laughed. 'I do know. Never in one place for more than a month at a time—no wonder——' She bit the word off, cursing herself for her tactlessness.

'No wonder I wanted a home of my own, you were going to say,' Lucy observed with a bitter little smile which softened as she saw the concern on her friend's face.

'Don't worry, Bella, it's water under the bridge now. Go on telling me about Matthew Fenn. He's not coming, you say?'

'No, he rang yesterday to say he didn't feel up to it. As I said, he's had a bad skiing accident and his leg's still giving him trouble. It was a hospital job, and although he's not in plaster now his leg's still painful.'

'Poor man!' Lucy explained with ready sympathy. 'I hope he's got someone to look after him .'

'I'm sure he has,' Bella told her firmly. 'We all know your urge to rescue lame ducks, but you're not to start worrying about him—or anyone else—this evening. You're here to enjoy yourself—or try to,' she added gently. 'Phil, pour us a couple of glasses, there's a love.'

They hadn't taken more than a sip or two before Bella's house began to fill up and any further thoughts of the absent Matthew Fenn were quickly banished from Lucy's mind as the party gathered momentum.

Bella seemed to have managed to collect together most of Lucy's available friends, all equally determined to give her a good time, assuming they were here to help her forget that the one person who should have been here to celebrate with her, her fiancé, was several hundreds of miles away. The news about the broken engagement could be let slip at some later date, Bella decided privately.

Lucy was just moving away from one group of friends to speak to someone else she'd spotted on the far side of the room when Bella pushed through the crowd to pull her back.

'Hang on a minute,' she said. 'There's someone here I want you to meet. I don't think you've ever met my brother Nick, have you? And if anyone can cheer you up, he can,' she whispered softly.

'The mystery man himself? Don't tell me I'm going to meet him at last?'

Bella nodded. 'I've actually managed to pin him down. He's just back from Oman and on the way to somewhere else equally hot and dusty—Abu Dhabi, Timbuktu. . . I don't know. Anyway, the main thing is that he's here.'

Lucy smiled up at the tall man by Bella's side, fair like his sister, and deeply tanned.

'I've heard such a lot about you,' she greeted him. 'You're in the oil business, aren't you? Always abroad.' Like Stephen, she thought, with a pang quickly suppressed.

Nick nodded with a cheerful grin. 'But if I'd known what I'd been missing all these years, I'd have come home a lot sooner—even considered settling down,' he added solemnly.

He took Lucy's outstretched hand and brought it with a gallant bow to his lips.

'None of that!' Bella reprimanded him sharply, giving his hand a playful tap. 'You'll have to watch him,' she warned Bella with an affectionate grin, 'he's just an old reprobate and he's got a terrible reputation. A girl in every port. . .or several, I dare say, if I know him, but

I've sworn him to good behaviour— for this evening, at least. Now, be good and look after Lucy, Nick, and get her something to eat. I've got something to see to in the kitchen.'

'Let's find somewhere to sit,' Nick suggested when he'd obeyed his sister's instructions and piled Lucy with a delicious assortment of delicacies from the buffet. 'Look, here's a chair. You sit there, and I'll sit on the floor. At your feet,' he added with a roguish glint in his eye that made Lucy laugh.

She smoothed down her skirt and spread the paper napkin on her lap before placing the plate on it.

'Pisces,' Nick observed knowingly.

'I beg your pardon?' Lucy returned in surprise.

'Pisces,' Nick repeated, biting appreciatively into a smoked-salmon sandwich. 'It's your birthday today, isn't it? March the tenth? So, you're a Piscean, the embodiment of all that's feminine, as well as things mysterious and dreamy. Even if I hadn't known today was your birthday, I'd have guessed at your star sign by the way you sat down just then.' He made smoothing motions with his hands. 'So meticulous and neat.'

He settled himself more comfortably at Lucy's feet, leaning against her chair and gazing innocently up into her eyes over the edge of his glass.

'Astrology isn't the sort of thing I'd have imagined a successful and busy oil man would be interested in,' Lucy remarked curiously. 'Or are you just pulling my leg?'

'Not at all,' Nick replied, his face quite serious. 'I guess it has something to do with sleeping under the desert sky so often. The stars seem much bigger and brighter there, somehow, and it's easy to become fascinated by them.'

'It's not something I've ever given much thought to— apart from reading those silly bits in some of the papers,'

Lucy grinned. 'But you think there's a lot more to it than that, do you? You take it seriously?'

'Definitely,' Nick asserted firmly. 'I've hardly ever met anyone who didn't have most of the characteristics of their star sign—like you, for instance.'

'So what's your sign?'

'Guess.'

Lucy shook her head, making her fine dark hair fly out round her face. She used both hands to smooth it back, adjusting one of the combs holding it in place, then laughed self-consciously as she caught Nick's knowing eye. 'I hate it when it's a mess,' she admitted, 'but I hadn't realised my actions were such a give-away. As for you. . .'

She considered the brown, good-looking face turned expectantly towards her, meeting Nick's humorous blue eyes with her steady gaze.

'Gemini?' she hazarded. 'Difficult to pin down, Bella said. I don't know. . .as I said, it's not something I've ever thought about.'

Nick laughed delightedly. 'Right first time—versatile, impulsive, and totally brilliant, that's me! But I'd much rather talk about you. What do you do for a living? Something for other people, I'll bet?'

Lucy pulled a face. 'It's difficult to explain exactly what I do. I sort of invented my job to suit myself. I suppose you'd call me an itinerant housekeeper. Housekeeper's what I put on forms, anyway.'

'A housekeeper?' Nick echoed in surprise. 'You're not my idea of a typical housekeeper.' He ran his eyes admiringly over Lucy's slight and elegant form.

'That's because she's not.' Phil was passing by, a bottle in either hand, and had overheard the last part of their conversation. 'Housekeeper may be what she calls herself, but our Lucy's a very superior, highly sought-after one, I can tell you. She's a cordon-bleu cook, a highly trained florist, and a lot of other things as well. She goes on short-term contracts to anyone who needs her to run their homes for a time—if they can afford her exorbitant fees, that is,' he added teasingly.

Lucy looked hurt. 'I only charge what I think they can afford. Sometimes, you see,' she went on to explain to the fascinated Nick, 'if a family is pretty hard-up but they need me to help them out of an emergency, I don't ask much more than my expenses. Others. . .' she shrugged gently '. . .others subsidise the poorer ones. No one's ever complained.'

'I should think not,' Phil commented warmly. 'There's a Lucy Ambleside waiting-list almost as long as Eton's or Glyndebourne's, and no one in their right mind would complain. Not if they ever wanted her to come to their homes again.'

'Wow!' Nick looked at her in mounting respect. 'So what made you start on such an unusual career in the first place?'

Lucy folded her hands on her lap and thought for a moment. 'I'm not sure. Something to do with wanting to be my own boss, I think. And I didn't want to be just a cook, or just a flower arranger. Then a friend needed me to help her out of a bad patch. . .and it seemed to grow from that. I suppose I like to feel needed,' she ended with a self-deprecating smile.

Nick nodded sagely. 'I might have known. A true Piscean woman, you are, through and through. A born home-maker.'

Phil put the bottles down on the mantelpiece behind him and squatted down beside Nick.

'Maybe you should offer your services to poor old Matthew Fenn. Did Bella tell you about him?'

'She said he was a business colleague of yours and that he was having trouble with a broken leg. Skiing, wasn't it?'

'Hmm. Quite nasty, I gather, and his regular housekeeper's had to go away for a while, so I don't know how he's managing. But he's very rich, so you could ask what you liked,' Phil added with a mischievous grin.

'He's not married, then, or anything?'

'Not even "or anything", so far as I know. No, I think he's quite alone, so I'm sure he'd appreciate your expert ministrations.'

Lucy's face clouded suddenly. 'I'm not sure. . . I don't think I want to commit myself to a new job, not just at the moment. There's something. . .' Her voice trailed off and her fingers strayed abstractedly to pleat complicated patterns in the edge of her napkin before she came to with a start to find both men looking at her with concern.

'It's nothing,' she told them quickly, anxious to change the subject before one of them began to probe too close to the ache in her heart. 'Just something I have to sort out before I take on anything else.'

Just then, to her relief, Bella appeared with a birthday cake, complete with candles, for Lucy to cut, and the moment passed. Toasts were drunk, then some people began to dance, and Lucy was swept away to join them, so it wasn't until much later when she was back home in her flat and getting ready to go to bed that Matthew Fenn came back into her thoughts.

She sat on the edge of her bed brushing her hair with the long, rhythmic strokes that gave it its deep shine. Matthew Fenn, she mused. . .where had she heard that name before? She tried to conjure up a face in her mind, but it was no use. The name remained obstinately disembodied—she must simply have heard it somewhere, though, for some reason she couldn't quite fathom, it seemed to set off resonances in the furthest recesses of her mind. Maybe Stephen had mentioned him—a business colleague perhaps?

Stephen. . . She'd tried so hard to keep him from her thoughts, but the wound left by the severing of their relationship was still raw enough for the pain to stab home when her defences were at their lowest.

All she had ever wanted was to be with him and settle down to make him a home, as his wife, which was something Stephen had never seemed to understand.

'Just when I've sorted this job out,' he'd say whenever she had tentatively raised the subject of their wedding. 'You know me—I like to concentrate all my energies on one thing at a time. Just let me organise things in Munich——' or Paris, or Los Angeles, or wherever '—and then we'll get down to discussing a date.'

But that wasn't the only thing that had made Lucy decide to end her engagement. After all, you could learn to live with a workaholic—even persuade them that there was more to life than computers and balance sheets.

She sat up in bed, hugging her knees, recalling the shock she had had that first time Stephen had lost his temper with her, when she'd glimpsed the raging jealousy that had lain dormant beneath his apparently otherwise well-balanced nature. She could hardly believe it at the time, but since then there had been other rows, culminating in the one they'd had just before he'd gone to Munich, and it was that which had tipped the balance.

Each row had seemed more violent than the one before, leaving Lucy feeling almost ill, and it had come to a point when she simply couldn't face any more.

But what effect her letter, enclosing his ring, would have on him, Lucy hardly dared think. Would he shut her out of his mind immediately, or come raging over to London to find her?

Lucy drew the duvet tightly round her shoulders as she envisaged only too clearly the terrible scene that would ensue. What she needed was to get away somewhere, until his anger had had time to cool down.

She closed her eyes and tried to sleep, but the face that swam before her closed eyelids just before she finally lost consciousness was not Stephen's, but the shadowy features of a man she'd never met. Matthew Fenn.

Over the next few days Lucy could hardly settle to anything. Usually, when she was between jobs, she enjoyed the break, catching up with friends and correspondence, cleaning her own flat and putting it in order, but this time was different.

Each time the phone rang, every morning when the post arrived she held her breath alternately hoping and fearing she might hear from Stephen. But there was neither call nor letter, and Lucy felt she was in a kind of limbo of uncertainty. If he was angry, at least she'd know where she stood, but this silence was worse than any rage.

Could he be too hurt to want to get in touch? That didn't seem likely, and yet. . .

'I just don't know!' she exclaimed wretchedly to Bella who, worried by her friend's hermit-like existence, had come round to persuade her to join her on a shopping-spree.

'I don't even know whether he got my letter. What shall I do, Bella? I don't think I could bear to ring him up and check—supposing he hasn't had it? Supposing. . .'

'Just stop supposing and come out with me,' Bella ordered her. I've got to get something to wear for my sister's wedding, and I need your help. Stop brooding and get ready. We'll go out to lunch while we're at it. There's that new wine-bar I want to try.'

Lucy pulled a face. 'I don't know, Bella. . .'

'No, but I do, and it's my treat. Come on—it'll be Christmas if we don't get a move on.'

'So what are your plans?' Bella asked as they were

finishing their meal with a cup of coffee. 'What's your next assignment?'

Lucy shrugged and stirred her cup meditatively. 'I'm not sure I can be bothered to do anything just at the moment. The universal helper-out-of-difficulties roles seems to have lost its appeal. Maybe I'll take a holiday and go abroad somewhere—Greece, perhaps. It should be lovely this time of year, full of flowers and not many people.'

Bella sat up straight and looked severely at Lucy. 'The worst thing you could do,' she scolded her.

Lucy looked up in surprise. 'What, go to Greece?'

'No, silly—go away on your own. I imagine that was your intention?'

'Hmm—I suppose so,' Lucy admitted.

'As I thought. And what would you do, all alone in Greece among the flowers? Brood, that's what.' Bella glared at Lucy as she answered herself. 'And get even more miserable than you are already. Am I right?'

'I might get picked up by a handsome Greek,' Lucy suggested flippantly. 'Let him help me forget my troubles.'

'Ha, ha, very funny. I can just see you,' Bella scoffed. 'No, I have a much better idea. You remember that man who wasn't able to come to the party—Matthew Fenn?'

Lucy nodded slowly. 'The man who's recovering from the skiing accident?'

'That's right. Well, he does *really* need someone to help him out, apparently. It seems his permanent housekeeper had arranged to go to Australia to be with her daughter who's having her first baby, and he insisted she went, but that's left him in the lurch. He's very particular about who looks after him, I gather, and he's had a whole series of people from agencies who've all been unsatisfactory.'

'How do you know all this, and what makes you think

I'd fit the bill, even if I took on the job?' Lucy asked suspiciously.

'Just a hunch—and I rang to ask him,' Bella replied airily. 'I pretended I was wanting to know how he was—which I was, too—and I ever so casually asked how he was managing, and said I'd see if I could come up with someone who might be able to help him out. Oh, I didn't give him your name or anything,' she added hastily, seeing the cross look on Lucy's face, 'but I thought it would open the way for you *if* you decided to give him a try.'

'Why are you so anxious for me to go and work for him?' Lucy asked curiously. 'If he's so particular, and has already got rid of all those people, he must be a very difficult man to work for, and I've got enough problems of my own at the moment without taking on his as well.'

To her disgust her eyes began filling with unwelcome tears which she dashed quickly away. Perhaps Bella was right. Perhaps she did need something positive to do to take her mind off Stephen, and if Matthew Fenn did turn out to be as difficult as she suspected from the quick change-over in staff, well, it would only be a temporary arrangement, after all. His own housekeeper would be back within a month.

'All right,' she said slowly. 'Give me Matthew Fenn's address and I'll go and see him. But I'm not promising anything, mind, not to you or to him.'

Bella's got a lot to answer for, Lucy muttered to herself as, with a mixture of curiosity, apprehension and growing misgivings about the wisdom of her action, she found herself outside Matthew Fenn's front door the following morning.

Why she hadn't telephoned him first to arrange an appointment, or at least find out whether he did still need a housekeeper, she couldn't have said, not even to herself, but this way she might catch a glimpse of Matthew Fenn before committing herself — or there might be something about the house itself to warn her off.

She stared around her to try and pick up some hints about the man she was about to meet, but nothing about the small and anonymous building in this quiet street off the Kings Road told her anything about the resident behind the black-painted front door. There were no plants, no fancy knocker, no individual touches at all.

Lucy sighed. Suddenly it didn't seem such a good idea, calling on Matthew Fenn out of the blue like this. The chances were he wouldn't need her anyway, and she might as well go home now before they both suffered the embarrassment of him having to tell her as much. Bella had made a mistake.

But even as she was about to turn away, her hand, responding to some deeper instinct, raised itself almost of its own volition and rang the bell.

There's no one here, Lucy told herself with relief as, after what seemed like an age of waiting, there was still no response. He was out, and that must be an omen.

She was already moving away to make her escape when she heard a noise inside the house and the door opened.

'Yes? What do you want?'

It was his eyes that startled her, even more than the aggressiveness of his tone. Penetrating, almost hypnotic, they seemed to bore into her very soul, and instinctively she dropped her own to study the pattern on the hall carpet behind him.

'Well?'

Lucy forced her gaze upwards again to meet his unmoving stare and smiled tentatively.

'I'm sorry to bother you, Mr Fenn—you are Mr Fenn, aren't you? Mr Matthew Fenn?'

Matthew Fenn nodded curtly. 'And you are?'

'Lucy Ambleside. You don't know me, but I'm a friend of Phil and Bella Robertson's.'

Now that she was here, confronting Matthew Fenn on his own doorstep, the whole idea of offering to help him seemed faintly ridiculous. The man before her simply radiated self-confidence, but she could hardly back away now, and lying wasn't in her nature. She'd have to tell him why she was here.

Lucy bit her lip, feeling his impatience mount as he stood, one hand resting on the door as though about to close it again, waiting for her to explain her presence.

'So why have you come to see me Miss—Ms?—Mrs?—Ambleside? And I'd be grateful if you'd come to the point. I am a very busy man.'

'I'm sorry—and it's Miss, actually. Miss Ambleside. I called to see you to ask if you needed any help.'

'You wondered what? What are you, some sort of social worker?' Matthew Fenn's strongly marked brows drew together in an irritable frown.

'Oh, dear, I'm not making myself very clear, am I? Look, I couldn't come in, just for a minute, could I? Then you wouldn't need to keep standing, and I could tell you how I thought I could be of assistance,' Lucy ended rather formally, cross with herself that this man's cold appraisal was making her sound pretty feeble.

Matthew Fenn went on staring at her, seeming to weigh her up, and shifted his weight, apparently with some discomfort, as he made up his mind with a barely suppressed sigh.

'All right, come in, Miss Ambleside. I can spare you a minute, I suppose.'

He turned without waiting to show her in, and called back over his shoulder, 'And shut the door behind you.'

Lucy did as she was told and followed him down the little passage into what was clearly his living-room.

'What a lovely room!' she exclaimed before she could stop herself. 'It's so big, and light, too.'

By knocking down part of a wall and creating an archway, the whole of the back of the house had been converted into one large room with big windows looking out not on to the patio she might have expected, but a pretty cottage garden full of shrubs and climbing plants. Entranced, she went to stand looking out at the clumps of early daffodils while Matthew Fenn eased himself, grimacing, into the chair he had obviously left to come and answer the door.

'Was it like this when you moved in?' Lucy asked him, 'or did you design it yourself? It really is beautiful, the garden and the room. One seems to grow out of the other.'

Matthew Fenn smiled, transforming his saturnine features so completely that it was all Lucy could do not to gasp with surprise, but the eccentricities of a wide variety of employers had taught her long ago to control the muscles of her own face as far as was humanly possible, so she merely returned his smile as he said,

'I can't take any credit for it, I'm afraid. But it is what made me buy the house. At the time I thought the garden would give me something to do, take my mind off——'

He broke off abruptly, the light fading from his eyes, and his hands moved in a dismissive gesture. 'That doesn't matter,' he said harshly. 'It's all in the past now, and nothing to do with anyone but me.'

One eyebrow rose infinitesimally. 'I'm sorry if that sounded rude, Miss Ambleside. I didn't mean it to, but it is the truth. Now sit down and explain yourself.'

Lucy sat down on the edge of an easy chair and put her bag on the floor beside her, smoothing her skirt down over her knees.

'I'm a friend of Philip Robertson's—he and Bella gave

that party last week you couldn't go to?' she added questioningly.

Matthew Fenn nodded but said nothing.

'Bella said you needed someone to run the house for you until your housekeeper comes back from Australia,' Lucy went on quickly, 'and, as that's my job, and I'm between clients at the moment, she thought I might be able to help you out.'

Matthew Fenn leaned back in his chair and steepled his fingers as he ran an appraising eye over her slight frame.

'Forgive me for saying so, Miss Ambleside, but you hardly give the impression of someone used to domestic work. I need someone experienced and professional, you understand, not somebody playing at keeping house to earn their pocket-money.'

Lucy glanced down at the smart suit she always wore to meet prospective clients, and flushed with anger.

'I am a professional, Mr Fenn, and highly experienced and qualified. If I'd come in my overall with my hair in curlers would that have convinced you of my credentials for the job? I don't think you would find there was much I wasn't prepared for or able to undertake if I agreed to work for you.'

She heard a quick intake of breath, and Matthew Fenn's dark brows drew together in a forbidding line as he stared icily across at her.

'*If* you agreed. . . That's very gracious of you, Miss Ambleside,' he commented in a tone heavy with sarcasm. 'And what makes you think I have any intention of wishing to employ you?'

'I don't suppose you have, not now,' Lucy replied cheerfully, able to meet his penetrating gaze directly now she had nothing to lose. She stood up and smoothed down her skirt, preparing to leave this disagreeable man to his own devices. Pocket-money, indeed! Who did he think he was?

'You obviously have made up your mind that I am totally unsuitable for the job, and I apologise for wasting your time. I hope you find someone soon to match your expectations.'

She began to move towards the door when Matthew Fenn spoke.

'No, stop—please.' The last word sounded forced out, as though it was one that came unnaturally to him, and Lucy, almost against her will, hesitated and turned to face him once more.

'I apologise, Miss Ambleside,' Matthew Fenn said stiffly, pausing a moment as though marshalling his thoughts. 'That was rude, and I'm sorry. Maybe we should begin again. Please——' he gestured towards the chair Lucy had just left '——come and sit down again. Your friend was quite right, I do need someone to run the house, and we might as well discuss the work involved now you're here.'

'You do have a regular housekeeper, don't you?' Lucy enquired. 'Bella said something about her having gone to Australia?'

Matthew Fenn sighed irritably. 'I'd already agreed to her going before this happened. . .' He waved impatiently towards his leg. 'But there's nothing out of the ordinary about the work here—certainly not for anyone experienced.' His lips curved in an ironic but not unattractive smile. 'All the things that keep a household—even a household of one—ticking over efficiently. The occasional small dinner-party, possibly, since at the moment I find it easier to entertain contacts at home rather than take them to restaurants,' he added with a grimace.

'Does it give you a lot of pain still?' Lucy enquired sympathetically. 'A bad break, Phil said it was.'

'Hmm.' Acknowledging human weakness obviously came reluctantly to him. 'It's better than it was, I suppose, but it's such a damn nuisance not being able to do all the things I want to do — and to have to keep going back to the hospital for physiotherapy. Such waste of time!'

He frowned angrily and beat one fist irritably against his thigh.

'Supposing we gave one another a week's trial?' Lucy suggested, hoping to defuse Matthew Fenn's rising temper. 'See how we get on?'

'When could you move in?'

'Move in?' This was something new and unforeseen. 'No one ever said it was a live-in job. I usually work from home. I don't make exceptions except for people I already know.'

She saw that infuriating eyebrow rise again. 'I assure you, you'd have nothing to fear, coming to live here,' Matthew Fenn said coolly. 'My intentions are strictly honourable.'

Lucy was annoyed to feel her cheeks grow warm. 'I never anticipated anything else,' she said stiffly. 'It's a rule of mine, that's all.'

Matthew Fenn smiled briefly. 'Rules are made to be broken, so they say, and, to be quite frank, if you can't live in you'd be no use to me. I need someone around all the time. I can't be doing with people coming and going all the time. It's live in or nothing. If you can't manage it I'd better contact the agency again.'

'I don't know. . .' Lucy said again, then stopped, biting her lip as Matthew Fenn looked at her, impatience at her indecision written on every line of his face. A new thought had just struck her. If she were to come here to live, just for a month or so, at least she would be out of the way if Stephen came looking for her.

Even so, she'd never made an exception to her own

rule before. Why, then, for this man? she wondered even as she heard herself agreeing to do what he wanted.

'All right,' she said reluctantly. 'I suppose I could, as it's only for a few weeks. When would you like me to begin?'

'As soon as possible,' Matthew Fenn replied promptly. 'Today? Tomorrow?'

The sudden smile Lucy had glimpsed earlier illuminated his face briefly, setting up a wholly unexpected quiver deep in her stomach.

'I could manage tomorrow,' she told him a trifle unsteadily. 'If that's convenient?'

Matthew Fenn nodded. 'In the morning, as soon as you can? Right. But there's one thing we haven't mentioned yet that I'd have thought would have been of considerable importance—to you, if not to me. Something you'd need to know before making your final decision?'

'I don't understand,' Lucy said with a puzzled frown.

'Your salary, Miss Ambleside. Or are you so unworldly—or so rich—that money doesn't matter to you? Your job isn't a hobby, is it? You did say you were a professional.'

'Oh, I see.' Lucy grinned. 'Yes, I am, but——' she hesitated. She could hardly tell this man of her habit of adapting her fees according to her estimation of her clients' needs and finances. 'But the money's not the most important consideration of my work,' she went on, hoping she didn't sound too pompous. 'What would you think if I asked. . .?'

She named a figure which she hoped Matthew Fenn would think appropriate—on the generous side, but not greedy, and he nodded.

'That seems quite reasonable, Miss Ambleside. So I'll expect you tomorrow, and I'll show you round then. I do have a lot of work to finish just now.'

He held out his hand, signalling the end of the interview, and Lucy put hers into it, feeling his fingers close round it in a hard but not ungentle grasp which was strangely reassuring.

Perhaps Bella's idea would turn out to be a better one than she'd first thought, after all.

CHAPTER TWO

IT WAS only when Lucy was back in her flat, standing in her bedroom and deciding what to take with her to Matthew Fenn's house, that she began to wonder what she had let herself in for, agreeing to move in with a man who up until a couple of hours ago had been a total stranger.

She sighed ruefully. She couldn't blame anyone else for what had been her own decision, and, in any case, she only had to stick it out for a week, if it turned out they really couldn't get on together, she and Matthew Fenn.

She sat there, mulling over her thoughts, for some time, until her reverie was disturbed by the ringing of the phone, and for the first time since she'd posted her letter to Stephen there was no thought of her ex-fiancé in her head as she went to answer it.

'Hello? Oh, Bella!'

'Did you go and see Matthew Fenn? How did you get on? I thought you might have rung by now to let me know,' her friend chided her.

'I'm sorry—it sort of slipped my mind. I was just sitting here thinking it over, actually.'

'You're going to work for him, then, are you?'

'Yes, I am, as a matter of fact. I'm starting tomorrow.'

There was a short silence while Bella digested this piece of information, then she asked, 'So what's he like, then, your lame duck?'

'Arrogant and irritable,' Lucy replied cheerfully, 'which explains why he's without anyone to look after him. He tries not to show it, but his leg certainly gives him quite a lot of pain. I agreed to try it out for a week to start with. To look at, he——' Lucy paused as she tried to find the right words to describe her future employer '—he's tall, dark——'

'And handsome?' Bella teased.

'Handsome?' Lucy repeated. 'Striking, I'd say. Very dark eyes that bore into you, and a pretty tough face—a tough man, too, probably, but I'll cope, I expect. After all I've got used to all sorts over the years. The only thing is, he wants me to live in. I didn't want to at first, but then I thought it might not be a bad idea, as things have turned out. Just in case.'

'Stephen?'

'Hmm. I still haven't heard from him, and if he did come looking for me—well, I'd rather steer clear of any unpleasantness, or a row of some kind, just until I've sorted myself out. Look, to be on the safe side, don't tell anyone where I am—except Phil, of course.'

It was late morning the following day when she again stood on the steps of Matthew Fenn's house, her hand raised to the knocker.

'I'd have thought you'd have been here before this,' Matthew Fenn said brusquely as he opened the door. 'I've been waiting to go into the office, and it was extremely annoying to have to wait around until you decided to put in an appearance.'

Lucy hefted her bag from one hand to the other, waiting for him to stand aside and let her in.

'I'm sorry,' she said equably, 'but we didn't arrange a time, and there was quite a lot to do in my flat before I left. I did tell you I don't usually live away from home,' she added, thinking it would do no harm to remind him of this favour she was doing for him, 'and you didn't tell me you wanted me early.'

Matthew Fenn grunted and turned away, leaving Lucy

to make her own way in and shut the door behind her. This was hardly a very auspicious start to their relationship, she sighed, but she had suspected he might not be the easiest man to work for, to say the least.

'I suppose you want to see your room,' Matthew Fenn commented ungraciously. 'Forgive me if I don't actually go upstairs myself. I still find stairs rather awkward,' he added, frowning, 'but your room will be the first one on the right, and you'll find sheets and things in the airing-cupboard in the bathroom. Oh, and there's a spare front-door key in the kitchen.'

He made his way into the living-room and called back over his shoulder, 'Now you are here, I'll call a cab and be off. I don't know when I'll be back.'

Not long after, a taxi drew up outside the house, and Lucy watched from her bedroom window as, without even calling goodbye, let alone asking whether she had everything she wanted, Matthew Fenn climbed into it and drove away.

Well, she thought, with a sense of relief, at least I've got the rest of the day to sort myself out and see what's what. She could explore the neighbourhood, too, and find out what and where the local shops were. This wasn't a part of London she knew at all.

Her room could hardly be called spacious, but the bed seemed comfortable enough, and there was ample space for her clothes and other belongings in the built-in cupboards, which also housed a wash-basin. After all, she didn't need a great deal of room, as she wasn't going to be here all that long—only until Mrs Portland came back—and if she and Matthew Fenn found they were absolutely incompatible her stay would be even shorter than that.

Lucy quickly made up her bed and unpacked, then, trying not to feel too much like a trespasser, went on a tour of inspection of the rest of the house which was to be her domain for the next few weeks.

There were three bedrooms upstairs, her own, looking out over the street, Mrs Portland's, reassuringly full of feminine clutter and family photographs, and Matthew Fenn's at the back, with a view on to the garden.

She paused on the threshold, looking round. In her experience, you could learn a lot more about someone by even the most cursory glance round their bedroom than from the rest of the house put together.

Cautiously, she stepped inside. Under normal circumstances, she was sure there wouldn't have been a thing out of place, that Matthew Fenn would be irritated by the clothes piled untidily on the chair, spilling over on to the floor, and by the crumpled duvet lying in a heap in the middle of the bed.

Her hands itched to restore the room to its usual state of orderliness but, apart from picking up what looked like a very expensive shirt and putting it on the chair, and tidying up his bed, she held back. Better wait until she was asked to do so than risk a reprimand for intruding.

The furniture came as a surprise, though. Somehow she would have expected him to have chosen modern, no-nonsense designs, but the two chests of drawers were elegant, bow-fronted pieces—Georgian, she guessed, and lovingly polished to show off the patina.

There were silver-backed brushes on one of them, and a selection of expensive after-shave and other lotions, but, Lucy was interested to note, no photographs either there or on his bedside-table, although there were books, quite a few of them—travel books, a couple of recently published novels and, unexpectedly, a well-worn copy of the *Oxford Book of English Verse*.

Lucy smiled. Matthew Fenn certainly hadn't given the impression of being a poetry-lover, but the sight of this particular volume by his bed reassured her more than anything she'd so far discovered about him. Somewhere, deeply hidden behind that aggressive exterior, must lie a softer, more sensitive side to him.

Lucy closed the door behind her and went downstairs to finish her inspection of the house. The living-room, which clearly doubled as a dining-room, to judge from the small, round table at one end of it, she had seen already, and the rest of the ground floor held no surprises. The kitchen, where she ended her tour, was quite small, but so well planned that it gave the impression of having more space than some of the much grander ones Lucy had worked in, and the cupboards and fridge seemed stocked well enough with basic essentials.

She decided to get herself something to eat, then go and explore the streets round about before she started to plan Matthew Fenn's evening meal.

She had no idea when he might be coming home, nor any clue as to his likes and dislikes, so for this first meal she decided to play safe and make a chicken casserole with salad and cheese—if she could find the necessary ingredients in the neighbourhood shops.

She was in luck there, at least. Just round the corner was a butcher and a small supermarket with what looked like an excellent delicatessen counter. Catering was clearly going to be no problem.

Or, at least, Lucy corrected herself later, it wouldn't be a problem if she knew what time the meal was likely to be. She looked at the clock—seven-thirty now, and still no sign of Matthew Fenn. With a sigh she turned down the oven to its minimum possible temperature, checked the baked potatoes again, hoping he didn't mind them pretty crisp, and went to sit down in the living-room, turning on the TV for company.

It was about an hour later when Lucy heard the

distinctive sound of a taxi drawing up outside, accompanied by raised voices and the slamming of doors. She got up quickly and turned off the TV before hurrying into the hall to open the front door for Matthew Fenn.

There had clearly been some sort of an argument between him and the taxi-driver who was leaning out of his window still shouting after him.

'Well, don't come running to me next time you break your leg, squire! I was only trying to help.'

He caught sight of Lucy at that moment and added for good measure, 'You might teach your old man some manners, love. I don't envy you if that's how he goes on all the time. If I see him again, it'll be too soon, I can tell you!'

Lucy moved her hand in what she hoped could be taken as a placatory gesture, and watched as the taxi-driver sped off, still grumbling to himself, while Matthew Fenn glared after him as he made his way up the path.

'Damn fool man didn't seem to realise I could manage perfectly well,' he growled between clenched teeth. 'Almost had me over with his stupid efforts to help me out of the cab.'

He limped up the steps and handed Lucy his briefcase.

'I expect he meant well,' she commented mildly.

'I can do without his sympathy—and anyone else's, too,' he said coldly, flicking a warning glance in her direction. 'I'm not an invalid—my leg's been broken, that's all, but if I ever set eyes on that maniac who tripped me up. . .'

He didn't finish, but his meaning was only too clear, and Lucy, who had been standing aside to let him precede her into the house, thought better of it and walked in ahead of him. Ungrateful old misery! Let him manage on his own! Her sympathy was all for the taxi-driver.

She put his briefcase in the living-room and disappeared into the kitchen, where she rattled the dishes rather more loudly than was absolutely necessary as she prepared to bring them through to the table.

At least the food didn't appear to have been spoilt by this long wait, and it all looked—and smelled—very appetising, even if she did say so herself.

'I hope you haven't got dinner for me.'

Lucy swung round to find Matthew Fenn standing in the kitchen doorway.

'Well, yes, I have. . .you never said you'd be eating out.'

'I got out of the habit of having meals at home after. . .well, never mind that.' Matthew Fenn's brows drew together over brooding eyes, then, seeing the tray laid with cutlery and glasses, the attractive salad in its glass bowl all ready to serve, his face softened slightly.

'I'm sorry. I should have told you. Look, you have yours—if you haven't eaten already?'

Lucy shook her head.

'Then we'd better have a proper talk about the domestic details of your work here. I obviously didn't make myself sufficiently clear when we were talking yesterday.'

His face lit up then with that rare and amazing smile, and to her annoyance Lucy felt most of her disappointment and irritation drain away as she smiled back at him. After all, how could he have known she would assume he'd be back for his meal? It was just a misunderstanding.

'I'll have my meal in here, then,' she told him, 'but perhaps you'd like some coffee? We could have it together, while we have our discussion.'

'That would be very nice,' Matthew Fenn told her, 'but don't hurry, please. Whenever you're ready.'

Matthew Fenn doesn't know what he's missing, Lucy said to herself as she tucked into the casserole. It was a pity she'd made so much, but maybe she could dress it up for another meal—if she could persuade him to eat at home. She hoped she could, as she enjoyed cooking and it would be a shame if she couldn't show off her skills.

'How do you like your coffee?' Lucy asked as she carried the tray into the living-room a little while later.

'Black, no sugar, thanks, and if you could put mine on this table, please. . .?'

Matthew Fenn was sitting in one of the easy chairs with his leg propped up on a foot-stool looking, Lucy thought, rather more tired than he had the day before, but she knew it was more than her job—if not her life— was worth to mention it.

She poured the coffee and placed his cup where he had indicated, then put milk into her own before sitting in the chair facing him, waiting quietly for him to speak.

'So we'd better work out some sort of job description, hadn't we, if more misunderstandings aren't to happen?'

'I think it might be a good idea,' Lucy agreed, sipping her coffee and looking at her employer over the rim of her cup.

'While you've been having your meal I've been doing some thinking,' Matthew Fenn began, then his eyes brightened as he, too, tasted his coffee.

'This is very good,' he told Lucy appreciatively. 'I couldn't get the last woman the agency sent me to give me anything but instant. Said she couldn't manage the real stuff—had some ridiculous notion about it being bad for you.' His lips curved momentarily. 'She even tried to persuade me to drink some revolting herbal rubbish. That was when I really saw red and told her she'd have to go.'

Lucy dropped her eyes. 'I believe some herbal teas can be very soothing,' she murmured innocently, then bit her lip, wondering whether she, too, would be shown the door. Could Matthew Fenn take a joke, even the most harmless one?

There was a moment's silence in which she began to fear the worst, then she heard the sort of noise which might have been taken as a sort of half-hearted chuckle, and she looked up to find Matthew Fenn's dark eyes resting meditatively on her face.

'I hope you haven't any intentions to try them on me, Miss Ambleside, soothing or not, or——'

'Or I'll go the same way,' Lucy finished with a grin. 'No, you needn't worry. The only way to finish a meal is with real, freshly ground coffee, as far as I'm concerned.'

'And for breakfast,' Matthew Fenn informed her. 'Lots of it, and very hot.'

'And what else?' Lucy enquired. 'Toast? Rolls? Cereal?'

'Toast and Cooper's marmalade at seven-thirty sharp. And no chat,' he added firmly. 'I get up at seven, have my bath, read the papers over breakfast and am out of the house by eight. At least, that was my routine before this damn thing happened.'

He scowled at his leg. 'Now it all takes that much longer. What I can't stand is not being able to drive and having to depend on taxis to get me about—like that fool this evening. God knows how long it's all going to take—it's so frustrating, and so unnecessary! And all because of one dangerous, stupid lout who wasn't looking where he was going. There ought to be a ban on people like him going anywhere on the mountains. I'd sue him for every penny he's got if I knew where I could find him!'

The dark eyes flashed fiercely, then the hooded lids dropped and his mouth clamped shut as though he regretted saying so much and allowing Lucy to glimpse his constantly simmering resentment.

Lucy looked at him helplessly. Whatever she said seemed to set him off, and she was scarcely any the wiser about what she was expected to do for him. She sat in a perplexed silence until something of what she was feeling got through at last to Matthew Fenn, who smiled drily with a small shrug of his broad shoulders.

'Now you know,' he said, 'I find any enforced restriction of my movements extremely annoying, and if you want to leave now. . .?'

Lucy shook her head. 'We said a week, and I'm not one to go back on an arrangement, but there are still one or two details to finalise, if we could discuss them now?'

At last she seemed to have caught his attention, and she quickly ran through the list of things for which she needed his instructions.

'I only want to make your life more manageable, and as comfortable as possible,' she told him. 'That is why I'm here; so wouldn't you like to try my cooking tomorrow? Unless you have a prior engagement, of course. And I won't intrude on your privacy more than is absolutely necessary. I'm quite used to making myself invisible.'

Matthew Fenn looked at her sharply as though he were really seeing her for the first time, and Lucy forced herself to hold his piercing gaze.

'I don't think invisibility is a necessary requirement for the job, Miss Ambleside,' he murmured, his dark eyes glinting suddenly.

'I did ask you to come and live here, after all, and yes, I'll come straight back from the office tomorrow and have dinner here. I'm sorry about this evening.'

'Is there anything you don't like or can't eat?' Lucy asked him, pleased at her small triumph.

Matthew Fenn shook his head. 'I like most things—except herbal tea, and nut rissoles, whatever they are. I've never actually eaten them, but that woman threatened me with them, so that was quite enough to put me off them for life.'

Lucy laughed and got up to collect the cups and put them on the tray.

'No worries there, Mr Fenn. I promise I'll not let a nut rissole over the threshold.'

She held out her hand. 'I'll wash these up and get off to bed—unless I can do anything else for you?'

Matthew Fenn took her hand in a strong and surprisingly warm grasp, holding it just a second longer than was absolutely necessary, and Lucy was startled by the nervous energy that communicated itself through his fingers to her own senses—a vitality that ran up her arm to quicken her pulses and bring with it a certain feeling of alarm as she met again those deeply unfathomable eyes burning into hers.

She withdrew her hand hastily and turned to pick up the tray.

'No,' Matthew Fenn said evenly, 'there's nothing more you can do for me, thanks. I don't sleep very well at the moment, so I'll finish off some work before I turn in. I hope *you* sleep well, though.'

'I'm sure I shall. Goodnight, then, Mr Fenn. I'll see you tomorrow morning at seven-thirty sharp.'

I hope I don't oversleep, Lucy thought, sitting on her bed to brush her hair. That would definitely *not* be appreciated, especially after the rather shaky beginning to their relationship.

What a strange man he was, so intimidating and yet allowing just occasional glimpses of less abrasive qualities to filter through the black cloud that seemed to be permanently settled on his stern features. At least working for him would be a challenge, she thought with a wry smile, as her mind went back to that strange conversation she'd had with Nick at her birthday party. Were Pisces people really as he'd told her they were? What was it? The embodiment of all that was feminine, home-makers, dreamy and mysterious?

Lucy laughed at her reflection in the mirror. What nonsense. . .and yet, maybe there was a grain of truth in his description. She couldn't bear to look untidy, and always did her best to dress as attractively as possible—not through any sense of vanity, but simply because that was how she was made.

Dreamy and mysterious were qualities she could hardly judge for herself, but she *did* like making people comfortable—which was precisely why she was here. To make life easier for Matthew Fenn, if only he would let her.

Once again Lucy found her thoughts straying to the man downstairs. Moody and irritable he undoubtedly was, but his accident and all that it had involved was enough to tax the temper of even the most easygoing of men.

But when he smiled—really smiled—the effect, as she already knew, was devastating. . .

What sign had Matthew Fenn been born under, she wondered idly? And, if she knew, would she be any nearer understanding the complications of his character? She doubted it, somehow.

One thing she did feel sure about, though, Lucy decided as she lay in bed listening to her employer make his way upstairs, some time later. She was as safe beneath his roof as she would be back in her own flat. He was, she was certain, the soul of honour.

The next morning, so afraid she might oversleep, Lucy woke long before Matthew Fenn was stirring, and, by the time he made his appearance at seven-thirty, the coffee was bubbling gently and everything else was waiting for him on the neatly laid table.

Scrupulously careful not to annoy him with unnecessary chatter, Lucy merely asked whether he had everything he needed, then, after what she took to be an affirmative grunt, withdrew to the kitchen and her own breakfast.

She kept well out of his way until she heard him ring for a taxi, then cautiously stepped out into the hall.

'So I can expect you back for dinner this evening, then, Mr Fenn?'

Matthew Fenn nodded. 'That was our agreement, wasn't it?'

'I was just confirming that you hadn't changed your mind,' Lucy said, feeling unjustly chastened by the sharpness of his tone. 'Or you might have remembered a previous engagement.'

'I'd have told you if I had,' Matthew Fenn pointed out with some asperity. 'I don't normally cancel arrangements without informing the people concerned. I should be back at around seven.'

So what had happened to cause him to go back on his word and fall short of his own high standards? Lucy wondered gloomily at eight o'clock that evening when Matthew Fenn still hadn't put in an appearance. If some crisis had arisen at work that needed his urgent attention, couldn't he at least have rung her?

She lifted the receiver to check the dialling tone, but the instrument seemed to be in working order, so there was no explanation for his silence there, and she couldn't ring him—not that she would, anyway—because she had no idea where he worked, nor even what he did.

'I should have asked him and got his office number,' she said out loud, feeling the need to hear a human voice after a day alone in the house, except for a quick trip to the shops to get the ingredients for this evening's meal— a meal on the point of being spoiled, she thought crossly. To say nothing of all her own efforts being wasted, for she had put a lot of time and thought into the creation of a meal she'd hoped would encourage him to spend his evenings here rather than in the restaurants where he had become accustomed to eating.

It was her job to make her employers feel comfortable and relaxed in their own homes, after all, and if she couldn't do that for Matthew Fenn she might as well pack up and go home.

Just as she had done the evening before, she went into the living-room and turned the TV on, trying not to think of the dishes waiting in the oven. Seven, he'd said he'd be back, and it was now—what? Getting on for eight-thirty and although, realising he might have been unavoidably detained, she'd not prepared anything that would spoil irrevocably by being simmered gently for some time, Matthew Fenn didn't know that.

He'd promised to be back, and told her categorically he never went back on an arrangement.

So what was keeping him? Lucy wondered for about the fiftieth time as the hands of the kitchen clock advanced towards the next hour.

Supposing it wasn't work, though? Supposing he'd had an accident or he'd damaged his injured leg and been rushed to hospital? He might have been knocked down by an impatient driver and be unable to contact her—be unconscious, even. How could she find out? She could hardly ring every hospital in London—there was no option but to sit here and go on waiting.

Nine o'clock came and went, and it was as Lucy was finally removing the dishes from the oven and turning off the heat, too anxious now even to eat anything herself, that she heard the familiar sound of a taxi engine outside.

She flew to the front door and flung it open.

'Mr Fenn—there you are! I've been so worried. Are you all right?'

Matthew Fenn paused and directed a hard stare at Lucy's anxious frown.

'Worried?' he repeated. 'Why should you be worried? Why this fuss? For goodness' sake, girl, it's a housekeeper I thought I had employed, not a nanny!'

A cold anger began to seethe in Lucy's brain, obliterating her usual calm.

'I'm not fussing, and if I'm worried——' She broke off as she noticed for the first time the two men who had just got out of a second car parked outside, and who were following Matthew Fenn up the path.

'What——?' Matthew Fenn began, watching the direction of Lucy's gaze. 'Oh, yes. My colleagues have just flown in and I've brought them back here for something to eat. I knew you'd have a meal ready.'

The dark eyes seemed to challenge her just for a split second, glinting with what looked like a hint of malicious pleasure, then, ignoring her, he walked straight on into the house.

The other two, more polite, stood aside to let Lucy go in before them, one giving a courteous bow in her direction that she wished her boss could have seen.

'I'll just get those papers, then you must stay for a meal,' she heard Matthew say as they reached the living-room. 'It's much too late to begin looking for a restaurant. It's all fixed. My housekeeper will rustle something up for us; now, what about a drink? Miss Ambleside, some ice, please, as soon as you can.'

Never, Lucy fumed to herself as she got the ice out of the fridge and put it on a tray to take through, never have I been treated so. . .so casually. Casually and rudely. And after only one day, too!

Perhaps it was unreasonable of her to expect him home somewhere around the time he had arranged, to think he might have the courtesy to warn her in advance of the trebling of the numbers she was to cater for?

Obviously she rated no consideration as a mere housekeeper, and a temporary one at that.

Lucy ground her teeth as she made two more avocado salads, thanking her lucky stars she'd bought extra ingredients that morning. Someone up there must be looking after her interests, even if no one else was.

It wasn't so much the fact that Matthew Fenn had brought his guests home to eat. It was his house, and he had a perfect right to entertain whom he liked. It wasn't even the fact that he hadn't apologised for springing them on her at such short notice which made her so angry. It was just his attitude, something she couldn't quite put her finger on—an innate arrogance bordering on contempt.

Sheer professionalism forbade her from showing any of her resentment at his high-handedness while she was serving the meal, which miraculously stretched sufficiently not to leave anybody hungry—except her, of course—and she was rewarded for her efforts by the appreciation shown her at the end of the evening by at least two of the men.

'Thank you for looking after us so well,' one of Matthew Fenn's guests said as she was handing them their coats. 'It was a delicious meal, and most welcome, especially as we've just had a long and rather gruelling flight from Hong Kong.'

Lucy smiled her thanks. 'It's been a pleasure, sir,' she said, 'and I hope you enjoy the rest of your stay.'

She said goodnight, then disappeared into the kitchen to tackle the washing-up. The dishwasher was already full, but there still seemed a lot to do, and then everything had to be put away—and, she realised, she was suddenly ravenous, not having eaten anything since midday.

She made herself a cheese sandwich and collapsed wearily on to the kitchen stool to eat it. Then, she promised herself with grim pleasure, she would go and find Matthew Fenn and tell him a week was seven days too long. Tomorrow she'd be packing her bags, and he would have to find someone else to run his house—and bully.

CHAPTER THREE

Lucy ate pickily. Now she could have something to eat, her appetite seemed to have vanished as quickly as it had come, and the cheese sandwich looked distinctly unappetising.

She ate about half of it, and was staring rather unenthusiastically at the rest, when there was a peremptory knock on the half-closed kitchen door, but before she had time to say anything Matthew Fenn pushed it open.

'I'm going up to bed now, Miss Ambleside. It's been a more than usually difficult day, and I'll need to be up early tomorrow. Check everything's locked up before you turn in, won't you?'

He turned to go, and that simple movement unleashed all Lucy's pent-up resentment that had been simmering away, ready to boil over. Not even a word of thanks for coping with the unexpected guests! She might not be a very important cog in the wheels that made Matthew Fenn's world go round, but she had her pride.

'Before you go, Mr Fenn,' she said coolly, rising slowly to her feet, 'there's something I feel I must say.'

Matthew Fenn stopped halfway to the stairs and looked back impatiently over his shoulder. 'Yes?'

'I realise this is your home, and of course you have a perfect right to expect me to cater for as many guests as you choose to bring back here, at however short notice, but I also feel I have a right to a little consideration. Just a phone call to inform me what was happening would have been a help; then at least I would have been prepared.'

Matthew Fenn swung round, wincing slightly, and stared at Lucy with total disbelief etched on to the harsh lines of his face.

'*You* would have been prepared?' He took a step nearer and, in spite of her determination to stand her ground, Lucy found herself flinching at the expression of cold disdain in his dark eyes.

'And who do you think you are, Miss Ambleside? My housekeeper, that's all. As I see it, your job is to be prepared for any eventuality. You are an employee, not a wife to be consulted about my actions.'

Lucy went very pale, but Matthew Fenn seemed not to notice the effect his words were having on her.

'If you're not prepared to be adaptable, Miss Ambleside, perhaps we'd better terminate our agreement here and now. I don't intend to reorganise my life—social or business—to fit in with your or anybody else's expectations. Is that understood?'

Lucy nodded and swallowed hard before daring to trust her voice. 'Quite, Mr Fenn. As for our agreement. . .'

She drew herself up to her full height and forced herself to meet his cold stare. 'I have always considered myself to be as adaptable as most people, and I have never had any complaints up till now about my work. Indeed, I consider it a matter of professional pride to fit in with my clients'——' she deliberately avoided the use of the word 'employers' '—requirements and lifestyles, but there is usually give and take on both sides, and, although I don't usually make a habit of breaking a contract, I am willing to make an exception in your case. As you are obviously of the same mind, I think it best if I leave tomorrow.'

'Quite a speech,' Matthew Fenn observed with cold sarcasm. 'And that suits me perfectly well. Just leave your address, and I'll see you get a cheque for the two days you have worked for me.'

With that he left her without another word, and seconds later Lucy heard his bedroom door slam shut.

Trembling, she turned back into the kitchen and subsided on to her stool again, too shaken by this altercation to think of tackling the rest of the washing-up. That could wait till tomorrow, before she packed her belongings and left this house for good.

Nothing now could possibly persuade her to stay here a minute longer than was absolutely necessary. Never in her life had she met a man so. . .so insolent. It was a wonder anyone would work for him at all, here or at his office, and as for Mrs Portland, she must be a positive saint if this was the treatment he meted out to her as well.

No wonder all his other housekeepers had left him! And no wonder there was no sign of any other woman in his life. It would be amazing if anybody could ever feel anything for him at all, except total dislike.

Lucy served Matthew Fenn's breakfast the following morning in total silence, matched by a taciturnity on his part that for once she was grateful for. If the only point of contact between them was their mutual antipathy, it was better they said as little as possible to one another.

'I'll lock up when I go,' she told him as he was getting ready to leave. 'And I'll post the key back through the letter-box. And you needn't worry I won't leave the house tidy,' she added stiffly. 'It'll be all ready for your next housekeeper.'

'I might not bother,' Matthew Fenn muttered as he shrugged his shoulders into his coat. 'More trouble than they're worth. I can probably manage better on my own.'

He left the house moments later, climbing into his taxi without so much as a backward glance, let alone a word of thanks or farewell.

And that was that, Lucy thought with a sigh of relief. She was never likely to see him again, thank goodness. She grinned ruefully to herself as she went back into the kitchen to face the rest of last night's washing and clearing up. That would teach her to go offering her help to strange men! Put the whole episode down to experience and forget it. . .and the man in question she told herself.

But she couldn't altogether suppress a pang of regret, too, at the way things had turned out. She didn't derive any pleasure from the feeling that she was running away from a job half finished. It wasn't in her nature to give up, whatever difficulties lay in her path, and there was only one person responsible for her sense of failure—Matthew Fenn.

One word of gratitude, even a smile, and she'd have been prepared to stick it out for the week at least, but no, the man was clearly devoid of every vestige of human warmth. He probably *would* end up coping on his own, and if Mrs Portland had any sense she'd stay on in Australia and leave him permanently to his own devices.

Lucy took a perverse delight in making sure everything was spotless and completely tidy before she began her own packing. Matthew Fenn would have nothing to reproach her with when he returned to his empty house that evening, she thought grimly.

She was just shutting her suitcase, checking she hadn't left anything behind, when the telephone rang.

'Mr Fenn's residence,' she said rather breathlessly after running downstairs to answer it. 'Can I help you?'

'Miss Ambleside?' a girl's voice asked, brisk and efficient.

'Yes—who's calling?'

'This is Mr Fenn's secretary, Miss Ambleside. He told me to ring you to ask whether you could meet him at the

Savoy this evening at——' there was a pause while she consulted her notes '—at seven o'clock.'

'The Savoy? Are you sure?'

'Quite. In the lounge, he said.'

'At seven,' Lucy repeated slowly, as much to give her time to think as to check the detail of the time.

'Are you there, Miss Ambleside?' the secretary asked impatiently after a long silence. 'What shall I tell Mr Fenn?'

'Tell him. . .' Lucy racked her brain wildly, wondering how she should respond to this totally unexpected invitation '. . .Tell him I'll do my best,' she said at last, thinking that wouldn't commit her irrevocably to turning up if she decided against it when she'd had time to consider properly. 'Is that all he said? He doesn't want me to bring anything with me—papers, or something he's left behind?'

It suddenly occurred to her that maybe he was just going to make use of her once more before she left his employ for good.

'No, that was all, Miss Ambleside. No other message.'

Lucy stood there for a long moment, weighing the receiver in her hand, while her thoughts whirled about her head. What was he playing at now? Why would he want her to meet him at the Savoy, of all places? Surely not for a purely social occasion? Not when he clearly disliked her so deeply.

Perhaps he wanted to settle up with her this evening, for some reason, or found he needed her for some task to do with his overseas visitors. Neither of these answers satisfied her, but they were the best she could come up with for the moment, and she still didn't know whether to accept his invitation or not.

Slowly she walked upstairs back to her bedroom and sat on her bed staring at her luggage, all packed and ready to go back to her flat.

Well, that was something she was determined to do, and nothing about his secretary's telephone call had made her weaken her resolve.

She'd leave as planned, and still have the rest of the day to think about how to respond to Matthew Fenn's strange request.

Lucy spent all day dithering. No sooner had she made her decision one way than she changed her mind, and it wasn't until late afternoon that she finally decided once and for all to accept what she was now almost certain was a kind of challenge thrown down by Matthew Fenn—unless it was an attempt at a bribe. . .Had he realised just how difficult it would be to run the house without any help, and thought he could win her over by an expensive drink?

There was only one way to find out.

She had a leisurely shower and washed her hair, then sat at her dressing-table to brush it, staring at her reflection in the mirror and wondering absently what Matthew Fenn saw when he looked at her.

Like his, her hair was dark, but, where his was thick and aggressively springing, hers was soft and fine, falling now to her shoulders before she pinned it back in the two combs she habitually wore.

Large eyes gazed back at her from beneath finely shaped brows, eyes which sometimes looked green, at others a misty brown that seemed to reflect both the light and her moods—ever-changing, like the waters of a mountain lake, an overly romantic boyfriend had once told her.

This evening they looked more green than brown. She'd wear her favourite olive silk blouse with a black suit, and some bright beads a friend had brought her from Mexico, to give an added touch of exotic colour.

She put the finishing touches to her face and slipped

into her clothes, then stepped back to view the full effect.

Not bad, she thought, as she adjusted the necklace. At least she looked suitably dressed for the occasion, and considerably more glamorous than Matthew Fenn had seen her up till then.

Although she set off for her strange date in what she had thought would be ample time, remembering only too vividly Matthew Fenn's cavalier attitude towards punctuality, Lucy wasn't altogether unhappy when her taxi ran into a long traffic-jam which held them up for a considerable time, so that she arrived at the Savoy even later than she might have chosen to do.

She walked briskly through to the lounge, and peered at the groups of people relaxing over drinks after work or before going on somewhere else. But there was no sign of Matthew Fenn, and she began to feel conspicuous as she stood alone, staring round her. Surely he couldn't be keeping her waiting deliberately—not after inviting her here specially?

Then a hand on her shoulder made her spin round.

'You're late,' Matthew Fenn observed. 'I've been waiting for you for half an hour.'

'Yes, I'm sorry,' Lucy said demurely, raising wide, innocent eyes to his face, where his ill-concealed impatience was clearly written, 'But there was nothing I could do about it. There was a huge hold-up, and the taxi got stuck fast.'

'I did begin to wonder,' he remarked, unsmiling, 'whether you were going to come at all—or whether you had decided to "forget" the time.'

'Neither of those things,' Lucy replied, secretly pleased that for once she had been able to give him a taste of his own medicine, 'but I must confess I was in two minds about coming. Your invitation was, to put it mildly, a little unexpected.'

Matthew Fenn made no reply, but put one hand under Lucy's elbow and guided her to the sofa he'd just left to come and speak to her, and, almost before she sat down, a waiter appeared looking expectantly at her.

'What would you like to drink, Miss Ambleside?'

'A dry sherry, please,' Lucy replied, hoping she looked more composed than she felt. If only she knew what was going on she might be able to relax and enjoy herself.

Matthew Fenn gave the order and leaned back comfortably to glance across at her, his eyes glinting in what might possibly have been amusement at her obvious puzzlement, but he still said nothing, and Lucy knew he was waiting for her to speak first.

'This is very nice,' she remarked politely, 'but I can't think you asked me to come here just to pass the time of day.'

Matthew Fenn drained the last of his glass as a fresh one arrived with Lucy's sherry. 'Very perceptive of you, Miss Ambleside,' he said ironically, 'but I thought it was as good a place to meet as any, and a lot more civilised than most.'

Lucy inclined her head in tacit agreement, and waited for him to continue. The ball was in his court now.

'It's also very comfortable,' he observed, 'and conducive to amicable discussions.'

'About what?' Lucy asked bluntly.

'About how to sort out misunderstandings, disagreements...that kind of thing,' Matthew Fenn replied lightly.

'And what makes you think there is any point in even trying to sort out our "misunderstandings"?' Lucy retorted. 'I thought we had said all that could be said on the subject last night. There's nothing more to add, so far as I'm concerned. A drink in "civilised" surroundings isn't likely to make me change my mind, I can assure you.'

'Not even if you were to get an apology?'

The deep voice was surprisingly warm, and the words spoken so quietly that Lucy thought she couldn't have heard them correctly.

'An apology?' she repeated. 'From you?'

'From me. Also, I thought an evening together in neutral surroundings might give us a chance to get to know one another better—and that can only be to the good, can't it, whatever the outcome?'

'Isn't it a bit late for that?' Lucy asked quietly.

'I don't know; we'll have to see, won't we?'

Their eyes met and held, and Lucy knew she was beaten. 'Just this evening, then—thank you,' she capitulated reluctantly, 'but I shall be leaving, I promise. I really don't think there's any point to my staying on—and I don't want you getting the impression I'm a soft touch,' she added drily.

One eyebrow flicked up at her ambiguous words as Matthew Fenn's eyes left her face and travelled slowly and pointedly the length of her body and back again to rest on her reddening cheeks.

'As I said, we'll have to see, won't we? And now,' he went on quickly, as though to forestall any further demur on Lucy's part, drink up, and we'll be off.'

'Off? Where? Aren't we staying here?'

'Not this time. I've booked a table at——' and he named a restaurant which Lucy knew from hearsay was one of the best and most expensive in London, though she'd never been there herself.

And now she was going to sample its delights with Matthew Fenn, a man she heartily disliked and up until a couple of days ago she hadn't even met. Life was full of surprises!

'I can see how this place got its reputation,' Lucy

remarked as she settled into her seat and surveyed the menu with an admiring and professional eye. 'The descriptions are mouth-watering enough, and if the food tastes as good as it sounds. . . Is it one of your regular haunts, Mr Fenn?' she enquired casually, intrigued by the fact he had chosen to bring *her* here.

Her host looked up briefly from his own perusal of the menu. 'Not regular, I would say, but there are occasions when it seems particularly suitable. And speaking of which,' he added, putting the menu down and leaning forward across the table, 'could we drop the "Mr Fenn"? It does sound a bit formal, seeing that this is a social occasion? What do you think?'

Again Lucy found herself gazing straight into that intense, dark stare, and felt her face flushing.

'I think I could manage that—Matthew,' she returned as evenly as she could, 'and I'm Lucy.'

'Good, that's settled then. So what are you going to eat, Lucy? Something more appetising than a cheese sandwich, I hope?' he added with a mocking twist to his lips.

Lucy grinned. 'Definitely. I didn't even finish it, either, but I'm hungry enough to eat the proverbial horse now.'

She settled, after agonies of indecision, on a fruit soup followed by fish cooked in a cream and wine sauce with an interesting-sounding combination of herbs.

'Will that be enough?' Matthew sounded disappointed as he ordered a more substantial meal for himself, starting with pâté and going on to a ragout of guinea-fowl. 'Fish never seems to me to be very satisfying.'

Lucy found herself about to file that piece of information for future reference, when she remembered with a jolt that there wasn't going to be any future so far as her job with Matthew was concerned.

'Fish is one of the most difficult things to cook

properly, I always think,' she told him, 'so when I go out I like to choose dishes I don't often try to do myself. Not that I've ever attempted most of these,' she added as she handed the menu back to the waiter. 'Though I wouldn't mind trying some of them out, so——'

'So long as there was someone appreciative to cook them for,' Matthew finished for her with a wry smile. '*Touché*, Lucy.' One eyebrow rose lazily as he studied her across the table, but Lucy refused to rise to the bait.

'It does make the effort more worthwhile,' she agreed, crumbling a bread roll in her fingers. Drat the man! Was he going to spend the whole evening making meaningful hints? Apparently not, to judge from his next remark.

'So tell me some more about yourself, Miss Lucy Ambleside,' he invited her. 'All I know about you so far is that you are what might be called an itinerant house-keeper—or possibly a ministering angel,' he added with a mocking glint in his eye. 'And that you take a pride in your cooking—a quite proper pride, I'm sure.'

Their eyes met again, the luminous and the dark, in which appeared a momentary gleam of appreciation.

'But you can't spend all your time working? What do you do when you're not looking after other people? Have you any other interests or does your job fill up your whole life? I can't believe that.'

There was that new, warmer note again in the deep voice, making Lucy wonder whether there weren't something more to his question than appeared on the surface, and she darted a wary glance at him, but couldn't guess at his meaning from his enigmatic expression.

'Nothing very startling,' she told him lightly. 'The same things as most people who are based in London, I suppose. The theatre, films, that sort of thing—and concerts, too. I. . .'

She paused, and Matthew, seeing her hesitate, leaned

forward once again to fix her with his piercing gaze. 'Yes?' he prompted her. 'You what?'

Lucy sat back and stared down at her hands lying still on the table, then dropped them quickly on to her lap.

'Nothing,' she said firmly. 'Nothing else. I was just maundering.'

Her greatest passion, although not a particularly uncommon one, was, for her, something too precious and private to be revealed to this inquisitive and comparative stranger. Only those closest to her knew about it, and Matthew Fenn certainly didn't qualify to be counted among those.

'I enjoy my work as much as most so-called hobbies,' she went on, 'and I suppose I'm very fortunate in that.'

She took a sip of wine and smiled wryly. 'One of my friends tells me that's because I was born under Pisces. Pisceans are apparently never happier than when they're involved in home-making.'

Lucy tilted her head on one side and darted a mischievous glance at her host. 'So what are you? Do you know?'

'Scorpio,' he shot back at her. 'And *my* friends tell me that's why I'm so difficult to live with.'

He spoke in a quite matter-of-fact tone, as though there was nothing wrong in being called 'difficult', but neither did he sound particularly proud of the description. It was just a fact of life—his life—and something other people were expected to adjust to.

'Scorpio,' Lucy mused. 'I'm not sure whether I know any other Scorpios, so I'm not qualified to judge whether they're right or not.'

She began finishing up the last of her soup, but her hand paused halfway to her mouth as she felt she was being watched, and looked up to find Matthew's dark eyes fixed on her face, as though trying again to penetrate into her very thoughts.

'Maybe that's all to the good,' Matthew observed evenly. 'Too much knowledge might lead to more discoveries than is good for you—or to either of us, for that matter.'

A tension, vital and unexplained, hung in the air between them. Was that a warning Lucy wondered, keeping her own eyes firmly on the complicated weave of the tablecloth, or merely a light-hearted rejection of the claims of astrology? She wouldn't pursue the subject now, but some further research into Scorpio characteristics might be to her advantage.

'You asked me about my interests,' she ventured after a short silence, 'but you haven't told me anything about yours, have you? I know about your skiing, but do you play other sports as well? And I don't even know what work you do—not that it's any business of mine, of course,' she added hastily.

Matthew did not reply at once, but leaned back in his chair and raised his glass to his lips, lingering over the gesture, which somehow became something more sensual than a mere act of taking a drink, and again Lucy felt a quiver—disturbing and exciting—of a purely physical response to this man's undoubted masculinity.

Up until now she had only seen him as her employer— or her ex-employer, she corrected herself—a man to whom she had offered her help in an emergency. A hard, difficult man, yet oddly attractive, too, when he wanted to be: she hadn't reckoned on his posing any kind of threat to her emotions, which were already in a turmoil following the breaking off of her engagement. The last thing she wanted was any further complication, and if her relationship with Matthew seemed to be hovering on the brink of a new development she must be on her guard. There must be no question of her getting emotionally involved with *him*.

Matthew himself seemed unaware of what was going

through her mind, and had turned his attention to his meal, forking up a couple of mouthfuls before answering her question.

'My free time, such as it is, is mainly devoted to sport——' as I guessed, Lucy told herself '—all sorts: squash, swimming, skiing, of course, and tennis sometimes. Whatever's on offer, I'll give it a try.'

Lucy's eyes instinctively strayed to the broad shoulders and straight back, the sinewy hands playing with his knife and fork, and sensed, even as he was sitting there, the latent athleticism of his tall and muscular frame.

She smiled gently. 'It must be more frustrating for you than most people being injured—even temporarily. And I'm not fussing,' she went on quickly, noting the warning compression of his lips, 'just commenting. I suppose you'll be having physio for quite a while yet?'

Matthew's face darkened. 'More waste of time, all those visits to the hospital when I should be working. That's why my schedule was interrupted yesterday. Good Lord,' he fumed, 'that hooligan has a lot to answer for, and if I ever catch up with him he won't know what's hit him!'

'You mentioned something about this hooligan before,' Lucy observed, hoping to defuse Matthew's pent-up anger by getting him to talk about his accident. 'Did someone ski into you, then?'

'Fool shot out from behind some trees as I was going past. The slope was particularly steep just there, and I was going too fast to stop.' His heavy brows met in a brooding frown. 'Stupid idiot! He must have seen me coming—must have! But I've no idea who he was or why he happened to be there just at that precise moment. But if ever I do. . .'

Matthew's hands clenched fiercely and a dark fire began to smoulder behind his glittering eyes, making

Lucy flinch back in her chair. Heaven help the stranger if Matthew ever did find him!

Lucy's Piscean intuition sensed his revenge would be swift and merciless, and she regretted having drawn him out on the subject. Far from alleviating his fury, she only appeared to have aggravated it.

Instinctively her hand moved towards him in apology. 'I'm sorry, Matthew,' she said helplessly. 'I should have known better than to remind you. . . Let's forget him for now. This meal's too good to let him spoil it.'

Matthew's eyes refocused on her face, and slowly his fury evaporated, the tension easing gradually from the taut lines of his features.

His hand clenched on the table, edging momentarily towards hers only to drop quickly to his knee.

'I'm sorry, too,' he said with an irritable shake of his head. 'No use harbouring grudges that have no chance of being settled, but if I had my way. . .'

Lucy felt she must steer the conversation into less troubled waters. 'Tell me about your work,' she invited him. 'What business are you in?'

'Computers,' Matthew said shortly, pouring the last of the wine into their glasses. 'Programming, software, consultancy, advising on systems, trouble-shooting—if it's anything to do with computers, you name it, we do it.'

'We?' Lucy asked.

'Well, me, I suppose,' he admitted. 'It's my own company. I set it up some years back, in a small way, then, after. . .' again a cloud shadowed his face, but he shook his head slightly as though to rid it of an unwelcome memory '. . .after I left the firm I'd started out with,' he finished.

Lucy felt there was something he wasn't telling her about that episode, but that wasn't her affair and she had no desire to cause him further irritation.

'I know absolutely nothing about computers,' she told him blithely. 'But my friends who do. . .' Stephen, she thought with a sharp pang that made the words suddenly stick in her throat, and she turned away quickly to hide the pain she felt must be visible on her face.

'My friends tell me I'm a complete idiot,' she went on not quite steadily, trying to cover up her onrush of emotion with a light laugh. 'I haven't a clue about that kind of thing, you see. They had a try at teaching me at school, but soon gave me up as a bad job, and since then——' she shrugged slightly '—I haven't felt the need to penetrate their mysteries.'

Matthew grinned. 'There's nothing so mysterious about them that a logical mind can't master.'

'That's it, then,' Lucy laughed. 'You couldn't find a more illogical mind than mine. I'll leave computers and their ways to clever people like you.'

The atmosphere between them had lightened now and the conversation stayed on wholly uncontentious topics until the end of the meal.

'That was just about the best food I've ever eaten,' Lucy declared contentedly as she finished the last of her coffee. 'Thank you so much, Matthew. It's been a lovely evening.'

'I'm glad you enjoyed it.' His eyes narrowed as they met hers, enigmatic and unfathomable, but he gave nothing away about what he was thinking as he called for the bill.

'I hope you enjoyed your dinner, *mademoiselle*, *monsieur*?' the proprietor, a grey-haired and dignified Frenchman, said as he ushered them to the door.

'It was quite delicious, thank you,' Lucy told him, smiling.

'Thank you, *mademoiselle*,' he bowed, twinkling gently. 'I hope we may have the pleasure of seeing you both——' he stressed the word slightly '—again, and soon, perhaps?'

Matthew levelled a cool stare at him. 'Perhaps,' he said non-committally. 'We'll have to see.'

He went out into the street, but Lucy stayed behind long enough to lay her hand briefly on the Frenchman's arm, seeing the hurt on his face.

'You'll have to forgive him, *monsieur*,' she said quietly. 'He didn't mean anything. It's his leg, you see. He's recovering from a bad accident, and it does tend to make him rather short-tempered, but I'm sure we'll come back one day. It was a really lovely meal.'

The proprietor's face lightened. 'I understand, *mademoiselle*,' he said conspiratorially. 'I hope *monsieur* will be himself again quite soon.'

Lucy caught up with Matthew outside on the pavement.

'Where have you been?' he demanded.

'Just having a word with the proprietor, thanking him. . .you know. . .'

'Hmm.' Matthew gave a grunt, then asked, 'So what are we to do now?'

'Now?' Lucy's heart gave an uncomfortable lurch. 'Going home, aren't we?'

'Home, yes—but where?'

Lucy stared at him uncomprehendingly for a second until the penny dropped.

'My flat, please,' she said firmly, and gave him her address. 'That's where I live. I took my things there this morning. I did tell you I was going to move back.'

'I see. And nothing's happened since then to make you change your mind?'

'Like what?' Lucy asked innocently, knowing she was playing into his hands, but unable to stop herself. Her pulses were beginning to accelerate under his unwavering stare, and automatically she put her hand to her throat to hide the tell-tale signs of her agitation, catching as she did so an ironic twist to his lips. Did this man miss nothing?

'Like having got to know one another better?' he commented lightly. 'I had thought this evening might have made you reconsider?'

'I've already said I've made my mind up,' Lucy reminded him with a touch of desperation, 'and I think I was justified in the circumstances.'

'Maybe,' Matthew conceded drily, 'and maybe not. But I had hoped we could put all that behind us and begin again.' His voice dropped and he took a step towards her. 'Is there nothing I could do to persuade you to come back, for the week we agreed on, at least? Not even if I promised to try not to be so unreasonable again, and told you how grateful I am for your help?'

He was so close now that Lucy was forced to tilt her head back to meet his eyes, deep-set and with a light in them she hadn't seen before, a light so intense that she felt it might burn her.

'I don't think so,' she said quietly, her heart racing now as she exerted all her strength to keep her body from swaying towards him. 'I'd rather go home, if you don't mind. It's too late.'

Matthew didn't enquire what the 'it' referred to, but turned away with a brief shrug to hail the next taxi that cruised by.

CHAPTER FOUR

THEY drove in silence to Lucy's flat, the space between them charged with Matthew's unspoken irritation at the frustration of his wishes.

Lucy cast a covert, sideways glance noting the set, unyielding lines of the strongly chiselled features in profile against the light of the streetlamps. To be thwarted by a mere slip of a girl must come very hard to a man like him, used to getting his way in everything. Even so, she could be stubborn, too, when she wanted to be. She was not going back to the Chelsea house, come what may.

'This it, love?'

The taxi-driver's voice broke into her thoughts and she peered out to see where they were.

'Yes, this is it—thanks.'

She turned to Matthew. 'Thank you for a lovely evening. I really have enjoyed myself, and I'm sorry if it didn't turn out quite as you'd expected—or hoped.'

Now she was about to leave him for good she could afford to be more forthright, but Matthew merely nodded then leaned forward to open her door for her, his arm brushing monentarily against her shoulder.

Again she sensed that surge of vitality communicate itself, almost magnetically, to her body, and her eyes opened wide in instinctive response to his touch before she scrambled out of the cab, almost tripping in her anxiety to escape from his proximity, but to her surprise and with a twinge of alarm she saw him climb out after her and lean down to speak to the driver.

'Just wait a moment, will you? I want to see the lady in, then you can drive me home.'

Matthew tucked a hand firmly under Lucy's elbow as they walked together up the path.

'You don't have to, you know,' Lucy said, trying to ignore the warmth of his fingers penetrating the material of her jacket to her skin beneath. 'I'm a big girl now, and quite used to looking after myself.'

'Not so big,' she heard him murmur softly somewhere above her head as she opened her bag to find her key. 'And these days you can't be too careful. London's full of villains, and I'm going to see you safely into the house. It's the least I can do.'

That strangely warm note sounded in his voice once more, and for a moment Lucy wondered whether she was being wise in letting him come into her flat. Had she been right in her initial assessment of him as a man of honour?

Circumstances had changed since she'd taken up residence in his house. She had been an employee then, whereas now. . . However their relationship could be described, it certainly wasn't the same. Matthew might even feel she owed him some sort of favour for the lavish meal he'd treated her to—and all for nothing, so far as he was concerned.

But Matthew gave no indication that he had the slightest intention of behaving less than properly as he walked slowly in behind her and waited for her to turn the lights on.

'Everything in order?' he enquired, looking round him with interest. 'I'll say goodnight, then—oh, there's a letter. . .'

He stooped and retrieved it from the floor behind the door, straightening up quickly with a sharp frown as he read the writing on the envelope.

'This writing. . .' He stared at it for a second before

handing the letter to Lucy, whose heart stopped beating before it regained its rhythm with a painful lurch.

The letter she had been waiting for had arrived at last, but there was no address and no stamp, just her name in Stephen's bold distinctive handwriting.

She was too shocked to notice the expression on Matthew's face as she tried to make some sense from the thoughts that whirled, confused, around her head.

No stamp meant the letter had been delivered by hand. Stephen was back here in London, and had been here, to the flat, to see her. If she hadn't accepted Matthew's invitation she'd have been here. . .But she wasn't ready for that, she thought wildly, not yet. She didn't feel strong enough, sure enough of her own emotions, to cope with the tirade, even the abuse, she knew she could expect, were Stephen to find her.

She must keep out of his way somehow until his temper had died down and there was only one way of escape that she could think of.

'Aren't you going to open it?'

Matthew's voice was strangely harsh, but Lucy had no time to stop and wonder why as she thrust the letter into her pocket and looked up at him with a wan smile forced on to her lips.

'It's only a note from a friend—they must have called while I was out. I'll read it later.'

She took a step nearer to the tall figure by the door and raised wide, luminous eyes to his.

'Matthew, I've been thinking. Maybe I was a bit hasty, walking out on my job like I did. I don't usually go back on an agreement, and I did say I'd give it a week, didn't I? I'm sorry. I guess I did behave unreasonably.'

She spread her hands in a gesture of apology. 'If you'd still like me to come back and keep house for you, I'll get my things and come with you now. Shall we give it another try—maybe for two weeks, rather than just the one, to give us more time to make it work?'

Stephen's letter seemed to burn into her flesh as she waited in an agony of suspense for Matthew's reply, willing him not to be too proud to accept her offer. After all, his request had been turned down once, and she couldn't blame him if he wanted nothing more to do with her.

She watched one eyebrow rise as he considered this unaccountable about-turn.

'That was very unexpected,' he remarked with no great show of enthusiasm. 'You didn't strike me as the sort of girl who'd blow hot and cold. I wonder what's decided you to make this generous offer so suddenly?'

There was no disguising the sarcasm in his tone, and Lucy's pale cheeks flushed.

'It wasn't sudden,' she maintained, not very truthfully. 'I'd been thinking it over in the taxi, but maybe it wasn't such a good idea. You might be better with another housekeeper—someone who doesn't keep changing her mind, and one who'll provide nut cutlets and instant coffee,' she added with a desperate attempt at a joke, but Matthew didn't laugh.

'How do I know you won't decide to up sticks again when the going gets tough?' he asked acidly. 'It's not what I expect from my staff, I promise you. Still. . .' He paused, his eyes flicking from her face to the pocket of her jacket and back again. 'Maybe. . .' he went on, frowning, 'yes, maybe it would suit me very well, in the circumstances. It might just work out, after all. . .'

Again he stopped, appearing to be gazing through her at something, or someone visible only to his imagination, before he pulled himself back to the present.

'Very well,' he told her coldly, 'go and collect your things, then, and I'll go and tell the taxi-driver what's happening, and wait for you in the cab.'

You couldn't blame Matthew for not welcoming her offer with open arms, Lucy thought, as she flung her belongings into a suitcase, emptying drawers and cupboards in a frenzied desire to leave the flat as quickly as possible. But he could have shown just a little more enthusiasm when he'd been so insistent earlier in the evening that she came back to look after him.

However, she hadn't the time to go into all that now. The sooner she was away from here the better. Only when she was firmly ensconced in the comparative safety of Matthew's house would she feel safe and even able, if the opportunity arose, to explain her change of mind to Matthew.

Only the opportunity didn't arise. The atmosphere between them was civil enough, but nothing more. It was as though Matthew was deliberately keeping her at arm's length, almost as though he'd realised how she'd used him, and the new understanding he'd claimed he had been aiming at the evening he'd taken her out to dinner had been decisively nipped in the bud.

Lucy was quite glad of this distance that now existed between herself and her employer. It was all she could do to concentrate properly on her job. Any other kind of complications, and her veneer of composure would have crumbled altogether, for her whole mind, since she had received Stephen's letter, was centred on his presence here, somewhere in London, and her fear that somehow he would find her and start berating her as only he knew how, even trying to implicate Matthew in what he would see as her betrayal of him.

One day, of course, she would have to meet him, she knew that, but she wanted to postpone that meeting for as long as possible, or at least until Stephen's temper had had a chance to cool down sufficiently for the two of them to be able to discuss the situation calmly.

But knowing him as well as she did, Lucy was sure that that time would not have arrived yet. Even going out to the shops became an ordeal, and she found herself peering round corners and looking back over her shoulders as suspiciously as a fugitive in a second-rate film.

Any of her friends would have accused her of over-dramatising, but then, none of them had any idea of what Stephen could really be like when crossed, and Lucy hadn't enlightened them. She'd never been one to tell tales or spread rumours, especially about the man she had been going to marry.

She hadn't told them, for instance, of the occasion he had tried to dissuade her from going to work for a man—an old friend of hers, as it happened—who was trying to bring up his three small children on his own after his wife had died. He'd had to go up North for his firm and was at his wit's end to know how to manage—until Lucy had offered to help him out.

'He's only after you for one thing,' Stephen had fumed. 'You can see through that sort of ploy a mile off—or if you can't you're a lot more gullible than I took you for!'

The more Lucy had tried to remonstrate with him the more worked up Stephen had become until he'd ended up accusing her of being in collusion with her friend—David, his name was.

'That poor woman's only just in her grave, and all you want to do is leap into bed with her husband!' Stephen had shouted at her, his face suffused with a scarlet jealousy so furious that Lucy had begun to fear not so much for her own safety but for his health.

'You've gone far enough,' she had told him quietly, doing her best to suppress her own righteous anger at his wild and unjust accusations. 'I'm sorry you don't trust me, but I'm going to help David out whether you like it or not.'

Of course in the end Stephen had climbed down, contrite and apologetic at what he'd said, but that hadn't stopped him flying off the handle on similar occasions until, in the end, Lucy had had enough, realising he would never change and beginning to dread a future spent either as a perpetual hermit or trying to defuse an endless series of rows.

And now, should Stephen discover she was working for Matthew—a single man—*and* living, unchaperoned, in his house... She dreaded the consequences.

'Is there something worrying you?' Matthew asked in barely concealed exasperation one morning when she'd burnt the toast yet again. 'Or is this——' he waved the burnt offering at her '—a not very subtle hint that you are regretting your decision to return here after all?'

Lucy flushed and took the toast quickly from him. 'I'm sorry, I'll make you some more. It won't be a minute.'

She made her escape into the kitchen, hoping he wouldn't pursue the subject, but she should have known better.

'You haven't answered my question,' Matthew observed on her return. He spread some marmalade on the new, warm toast and crunched into it with an approving nod. 'That's better, thanks. Well?'

Lucy sat down and stared at her hands. 'There is something on my mind—a slight personal problem. I'm sorry if I've let it show—and for the toast,' she added ruefully. 'I'll try to concentrate a bit harder from now on.'

'Anything I can help with?' Matthew stopped eating and directed his penetrating gaze at her. 'A trouble shared...and all that? Someone bothering you?'

Lucy shook her head. For almost the first time since

they had met she heard a note of real sympathy in his voice, and she almost weakened enough to confide some of her anxieties, at least, to him, but held back at the last moment.

'No, thanks,' she said with a grateful smile. 'It's kind of you to offer, but it's something only I can sort out—in time. . .'

Her eyes clouded momentarily, then she dragged her thoughts back to more current problems.

'Will you be in this evening? Anything particular you'd like me to cook?'

Matthew pulled out his diary and perused it thoughtfully.

'Don't lay on anything special,' he told her. 'It's quite likely I'll be out—so you can forget me for a while and concentrate on your own affairs.'

Was it her imagination, or was there a slight but significant stress on that last word? Had Matthew once again got through her defences and glimpsed something of what was troubling her—or was it merely an inspired guess?

The latter seemed the more likely, Lucy decided later on as she puzzled over the question. After all, it wouldn't be surprising or unusual for a single, unattached—so far as Matthew knew—girl to have relationship problems.

And now here she was, all her work done and with the best part of a day to herself. How should she spend it?

Normally she would have had no difficulty in finding all sorts of things to do and people she could go to see, but at the moment, still unsure if Stephen was still around, she simply wasn't courageous enough to venture out alone, just in case. . .

Then, right on cue, the telephone rang.

'Hello, Mr Matthew Fenn's residence, can I help you?'

'Lucy?'

'Oh, Bella! How lovely!'

'That was very heartfelt. Everything OK there, is it?' Bella asked suspiciously.

'Yes, fine,' Lucy asserted. 'It's just. . .look, there isn't any chance of seeing you today, at your place, is there? Matthew's out this evening and I've got a whole day to myself. I was wondering what to do when you rang.'

'You must be psychic,' Bella laughed. 'The reason I rang was to find out if you could possibly come over this evening. Nick announced last night that he's off again in a day or two, and I'm trying to organise a farewell dinner. Can you come, then?'

'I couldn't come and help, too, could I?' Lucy begged. 'I really am at a loose end, and I don't want to go back to my flat,' she added in the sort of tone that made Bella prick up her ears with interest.

She made no comment, however, merely saying she'd be delighted to have Lucy's assistance as well as a good gossip.

'And if there's anything you want to tell me about,' she ended cheerily, 'I'm a good listener, don't forget. And your best friend.'

'There is something bothering you, isn't there?' Bella asked later that day as she looked at Lucy closely, noting the shadow behind the green eyes. 'Is it Matthew Fenn? I'd give the job up if you're not happy working for him. It's all my fault—I never can resist the chance to interfere.'

Lucy smiled wanly. 'No, it's nothing to do with Matthew. He's——' she paused, frowning '—he's not exactly the easiest person I've ever worked for, but I've only got to stay there for another couple of weeks or so, and I guess I can put up with him till then.'

'So what *is* the matter?' Bella persisted. 'I know you too well, Lucy Ambleside, for you to be able to pull the wool over my eyes.'

'It's Stephen,' Lucy blurted out. 'I got a letter from him, telling me he had to see me, and that he wasn't going to accept my decision without a fight. . .and that's what I'm afraid of.'

Bella stared at her, shocked.

'Really afraid? Yes, you are, aren't you? He's never threatened you, has he?'

'Not physically. But he always wants his own way, and whenever I've tried to stand up to him. . .'

How could she describe the icy rage that could transform Stephen's normally open and pleasant features into a mask of cold fury when he felt his wishes were being thwarted?

'I've never told anyone before,' Lucy said slowly, 'but Stephen is a very jealous man. And after. . .well, I suddenly couldn't take any more. I know I ought to see him, I owe him that much, and one day I will, but not till he's had a chance to cool down.'

'Jealous? Stephen?' Bella stared at her in amazement. 'But he always seemed so rational. Oh, love, that's terrible. And of you, of all people. He must be out of his mind.'

Lucy smiled at her gratefully. 'Thank you for the vote of confidence,' she said, then sat down with a heavy sigh. 'I have to admit it came as a shock to me, too, the first time. I tried to dismiss it as a flash in the pan. Then, when I realised it wasn't, I thought I could change him. . .convince him he could trust me——' She broke off with a bitter laugh. 'It's happened once too often, though, him flying off the handle and accusing me of— well, you can imagine. Think of how many attractive men I must meet in the course of my work,' she added ironically.

'Don't you think it might have got better once you were married? No, I suppose not,' Bella answered herself. 'But why did you finally break it off? Was there a last straw?'

'Something like that,' Lucy admitted, staring with unseeing eyes out of the window. 'You know he's been in Munich?'

Bella nodded.

'Well, I thought it would be nice to go out there when my last job finished. I could see Stephen and visit the Schmidts, the German family I worked for two or three years back. Herr Schmidt worked at the embassy then, but he's retired now and they've often asked me to go out on a visit. When I mentioned it to Stephen he got into one of his rages and accused me of wanting to see Herr Schmidt because—well, I won't go into it, and if I hadn't been so hurt I might even have found it funny! Herr Schmidt is over sixty and must weigh at least twenty stone!'

She looked helplessly at Bella. 'I discovered then that the reason Stephen never wanted me with him when he was abroad hadn't anything to do with his work. It was simply because he couldn't be sure there wasn't some other devious motive behind my wanting to visit him. I've worked for various foreign families over the years, you see, and he knows I liked some of them very much, including the men.'

'That's outrageous!' Bella cried. 'He really must be mad! No, you couldn't possibly go ahead with the marriage, I can see that. And if there's anything Phil and I can do to help, just let us know. The very idea!'

Her face was a positive study in disapproval, and Lucy burst out laughing.

'Come on, let's forget about Stephen and get on with these desserts. You've heard quite enough about my troubles for now, but thanks for listening. You've helped me get it all more into proportion. Poor old Matthew's been getting a raw deal these past few days.'

* * *

'I gather from Bella she's been keeping you busy in the kitchen all day,' Nick grinned that evening as they were taking their places at the table. 'I'm very glad I'm getting the chance to sample your culinary skills at last.'

'Before you go back to the desert and your stars?' Lucy smiled, remembering their previous conversation.

'That's right, Miss Pisces,' Nick nodded, flicking a glance at the tidily spread napkin on Lucy's lap. His grin changed to a smile of appreciation as his eyes travelled slowly upwards till they reached her hair, smooth and neatly confined in the customary two combs at the back of her head.

'You're going to tell me again how typical I am of my star sign,' Lucy sighed resignedly. 'The born home-maker— or in my case, housekeeper,' she added with an uncharacteristic tinge of bitterness. 'All feminine, not a hair out of place...utterly predictable.'

'Oh no, not at all,' Nick protested. 'All feminine, certainly, but as for predictable...'

He leaned forward suddenly and gazed into Lucy's surprised eyes. 'You haven't done your research thoroughly enough, Miss Ambleside,' he told her gravely, 'or you'd know there's another side to Pisces. The fish, swimming in mysterious depths, dreamy, mystical, imaginative. The changing lights in your eyes tell it all.'

Lucy became aware that the room had fallen silent as her friends were drawn into this odd and strangely disturbing conversation, and she gave a light laugh.

'Just coincidence,' she shrugged dismissively, 'and, even if it weren't, I'm not sure I want to be known as a typical anything. How about me as an individual?'

'You are just fine,' Bella reassured her, 'and Nick's only riding his hobby-horse. If you ask me, the sooner he leaves his beloved desert and comes back to civilisation for good the better. Come on, Phil, our glasses are empty.'

SHADOW ON THE SEA

Watching Phil circulate with the wine, Lucy's mind went back to her dinner-date with Matthew, and impulsively she turned back to Nick.

'What do you know about Scorpio people?' she asked him. 'Are they supposed to be difficult to live with?'

The smile on Nick's still tanned face faded, to be replaced by a look of extreme wariness.

'Scorpio?' he repeated slowly. 'Difficult. . .that's one way of describing it, I suppose. Why, who do you know who's a Scorpio?'

'The man I'm working for, Matthew Fenn. He says his friends have told him that's why he's. . .well, difficult.'

'As well they might,' Nick agreed. 'And moody, and thoroughly awkward. Also. . .' He stopped, his eyes narrowing as they took in Lucy's expression of growing alarm, not altogether feigned.

'They're not all bad,' he conceded. 'Scorpio people are capable of tremendous loyalty. It's only if they feel they've been slighted in some way, or offended, that you have to watch out. Still, you're not likely to do that, are you?'

'Only by burning the toast,' Lucy grinned. 'I must be careful not to do it too often, obviously, but he didn't seem to bear me any grudge about it.'

'That's a relief,' Nick said with mock gravity. 'Burnt toast is a capital crime to some people.'

Just then Lucy's other neighbour asked her a question about her work, steering the conversation into other channels, and it wasn't until Lucy was saying goodbye that the subject was raised again.

'Look after yourself, Miss Pisces,' Nick said, stooping to place a quick kiss on Lucy's cheek. 'Take care with the breakfast, and don't forget scorpions have a deadly sting.'

'Forewarned is forearmed,' Lucy assured him cheerfully. 'I shall be on my guard, never fear.'

But none of Nick's warnings prepared her for the onslaught which was awaiting her.

'Where the hell have you been?'

Almost before Lucy had got through the front door of Matthew's house he was there, towering over her, his face dark and furious.

'I came back here, expecting a meal, and there was nothing to eat and no sign of you. You hadn't even left a note to say where you were. Or who you were with.'

Lucy stared at him, dumbfounded. 'Who I was with?' she repeated slowly. What right had he to know who she saw in her spare time? 'I don't think that's any of your business,' she told him frigidly, 'and, as for my not being here, you said you'd be out this evening. I assumed. . .'

'"Assumed?" What right had you to "assume"? I employ you to look after me, Miss Ambleside, not to go gallivanting off whenever you feel like it. You've been out for the whole day, haven't you?' he shot at her accusingly. 'I know, because I tried to get in touch with you earlier on. And you still haven't answered my other question. Who have you been with all this time?'

'Employing me as your housekeeper does not give you the right to interrogate me about where I've been or who I've been seeing, but, as you're clearly so concerned for my well-being,' Lucy went on with a sarcasm that matched his own, 'I shall merely inform you that I was with my friends Phil and Bella. You can ring them yourself to check, if you doubt my word.'

Lucy's heart had begun to pound uncomfortably as she forced herself to stand her ground before his menacing figure.

'I'm sorry if it was inconvenient, and if I'd known

you'd had a change of plan, I wouldn't have gone—not for so long, anyway.'

'Of course it was inconvenient,' Matthew stormed. 'You've led me to believe I could depend on you, but I've been disappointed, Miss Ambleside. Gravely disappointed.'

Lucy undid her coat and moved towards the kitchen door. 'Did you have something to eat, Mr. Fenn?' It was clearly back to a formal relationship so far as he was concerned. 'Or would you like me to get you something now?'

Matthew's hand waved impatiently as he turned to walk back to the living-room. 'I'm quite capable of rustling up something for myself when necessary. Though it's kind of you to enquire,' he added with a sarcastic twist of his lips. 'And next time you decide to take yourself off for the day, kindly have the courtesy to let me know.'

'Unless you'd prefer that I leave altogether,' Lucy suggested with icy politeness, all memory of Nick's warning vanishing from her thoughts. 'I can pack now, if you wish. I'm sure you'll be able to find someone else you *can* rely on until Mrs Portland comes back.'

Matthew paused in the doorway, and Lucy saw his head go up as his shoulders tensed.

'As you please,' he rasped, the chill in his tone at least as arctic as her own. 'Just have the consideration to let me know what you decide, will you?'

With that, he shut the door behind him, leaving Lucy staring after him with mingled dismay and anger.

What was she to do now?

She walked up the stairs and slumped on to the edge of her bed.

This man, Matthew Fenn, seemed to have an unnerving knack of making her act totally out of character. Why couldn't she have tried to smooth things down, pour oil on the distinctly troubled waters when she'd seen how angry he was?

Where was her usual calm efficiency? And what had happened to the natural composure that over the years had helped her cope with people at least as demanding as the man downstairs?

The break-up with Stephen, followed by his letter and the constant nagging fear of meeting him must have upset her more than she had realised.

She should have taken that holiday she'd intended to have before Bella had persuaded her to take this job. She did need a complete break.

Lucy got up and wandered over to the window, staring out at the stars shining faintly above the lamp-lit street. She *would* go away, maybe not as far as Nick's desert, but somewhere miles away from these men who were causing her so much hassle.

She'd tell Matthew tomorrow morning—no point in hanging on here any longer—and suggest he start looking for another housekeeper. Then she'd pack her bags and drop in to the first travel agents' she came to, and see what took her fancy.

That decision made, Lucy felt a great weight lift from her heart, and when sleep finally came it was deeper and more untroubled than it had been for weeks.

CHAPTER FIVE

'MR FENN —Matthew?' Lucy began as she poured his breakfast coffee the following morning. 'I've come to a decision. May I say something?'

Matthew barely looked up from the letter he was reading, acknowledging her words with an almost inaudible grunt.

'Matthew?' Lucy spoke a little louder this time, determined to have her say before her resolve weakened.

'Yes? What is it?' With a sigh of impatience Matthew sat back and stared at her, unblinking.

'About yesterday. . . I do understand that you felt you had a right to expect me to be here when you came home, but it was an honest mistake on my part, I assure you. I did think you would be out for the evening.

'As for the other things you said. . .' Lucy grasped the back of the chair in front of her, and went on doggedly '. . .I *don't* think you had any right to interrogate me about where I'd been.'

She had his attention now, and their eyes locked in a direct confrontation of wills. 'It's clear to me that we're never likely to get on, and to avoid any further disagreements I think it best if I leave after all. I'm sorry, but I can't think of any other way out. Maybe I shouldn't have taken the job in the first place. What I need is a complete break. I do have some personal problems which need to be sorted out,' she ended, not quite steadily.

'Running away never solved anything,' Matthew observed coolly.

'No,' Lucy conceded quietly, resolved not to let him ruffle her again. 'And I'm not running away. I just want time to myself—to think. I'm sorry if I'm letting you down, but I think it's for the best. For both of us.'

'How do you know what's best for me? A touch arrogant, wouldn't you say?' With a gesture of pure irritation Matthew drained his coffee-cup, which he then cracked down on to the saucer so sharply that Lucy winced.

'I should have thought you'd have preferred to be looked after by someone you felt you could rely on,' Lucy said evenly, 'and it won't be for long, will it? Mrs Portland will be back in a couple of weeks.'

'No. She won't.'

Matthew rapped the letter lying by his plate and glared fiercely up at her. 'This letter... Apparently, Mrs Portland's daughter needs her for a while longer, and she wants to stay in Australia another fortnight at least, maybe a month.'

'I don't see that that changes anything,' Lucy told him stubbornly. 'You can get someone from the agency for a month just as easily as for a couple of weeks. You don't need me.'

'That's where you're wrong!'

Lucy had begun clearing the table so as to give her the excuse she needed not to have to attempt to hold his gaze, but his words halted her in her tracks as Matthew pushed back his chair and stood for a moment staring down at her with that piercing look she'd got to know so well yet never felt able to meet for more than a second or two.

'Supposing I told you I wasn't prepared to let you leave me in the lurch yet again? You offered to stay on for two weeks, if you recall?' he went on, his mouth curving in an ironic smile, 'and I feel inclined to hold you to that. You can't go on breaking agreements whenever you feel like it, Miss Ambleside, whatever your personal problems.'

Stunned, Lucy stared at him. Whatever reaction she had expected from her ultimatum, it certainly hadn't been this.

'But I. . .' she began.

'But nothing.' Matthew waved a peremptory hand in dismissal of her outraged protest. 'Our agreement stands, so far as I'm concerned. It might not hold up in a court of law, I grant you, though I don't imagine you'd go that far to get your way. . .'

'You can't keep me a prisoner here,' Lucy declared hotly.

'Of course not,' Matthew replied impatiently, 'and if you insist on leaving, of course I can't stop you, though I doubt if it would do your reputation much good if prospective clients discovered you weren't quite so reliable as they'd been led to believe.'

'You wouldn't——?' Lucy began, but again Matthew brushed her words aside.

'And in any case, we won't be here. Do you drive?'

Lucy sat down abruptly, her eyes wide with astonishment. 'Drive?'

'That's right,' Matthew returned brusquely, collecting his briefcase and beginning to move towards the door. 'As I said, I do need you—to drive me to Northumberland.'

'Northumberland?' She was so taken aback, all she could do was repeat Matthew's words.

'Yes, Northumberland. I have a house there, near the coast. I bought it for——' He broke off, frowning, and Lucy saw his hand clench by his side as he went on, 'Never mind that. Let's just say I have a sudden and urgent desire to visit it. I usually go up for a day or two after the winter to check everything's in order, and I'd thought of going tomorrow. If it's convenient, of course?' he added with a courteous smile that Lucy knew better than to take on trust. 'I realise it's a long way but, as you know, for me, driving is out of the question at the moment. So what do you say?'

His lips twitched with amusement as he studied her startled expression, then for a moment his eyes seemed to soften.

'There is one thing you might consider,' he added more gently. 'Northumberland is a long way from London, and very quiet. Very suitable, I'd have thought, for sorting out whatever problems have been worrying you.'

'Yes, I suppose so.' That was true, at least. Stephen would never find her there, and by the time she came back to London it was more than likely he'd have gone abroad again.

'You do drive, I suppose?'

'What. . .? Oh, yes. I quite enjoy it, actually.'

Matthew's eyebrows rose slightly. 'You're full of surprises, aren't you?' he murmured, and his lips curved into a faint smile. 'And it wouldn't be too far?'

'No, I don't suppose so. . .' Her words trailed off into a sigh as she realised that once again Matthew seemed all set to direct her actions along a path of his own devising. Ever since they'd met he'd managed to get his own way. Why did she let him, and why didn't she make a stand now to act on her own decision before it was too late? Why was she even hesitating?

But even as she was framing the words of refusal, she heard herself say, as though from a great distance, 'No, it's not too far.'

'That's settled then,' Matthew said firmly. 'I'll have my car brought round later, and we can be off tomorrow, first thing.'

'Tomorrow,' Lucy echoed feebly.

'That's right. That should give you time to tidy up here and collect your things. Warm clothes, don't forget,' he warned her. 'You won't be needing your bikini. And then we can leave early in the morning to avoid the rush. We could be there by lunchtime.'

She must be mad, Lucy kept telling herself as she rushed about preparing for this unexpected trip. And not only unexpected. Unwanted, as well. Why, she asked herself over and over again, had she allowed this to happen?

By this time she should have shaken the dust of this place from her feet forever, planning her holiday in Greece, Italy, Portugal. . .somewhere warm and anonymous, and, instead, not only was she committed to driving herself and Matthew hundreds of miles up the A1 to a place she didn't particularly want to go to, but, even worse, she had once again let him bulldoze her into going along meekly with his wishes. Why hadn't she had the courage of her own convictions and left him, as she'd vowed to do?

She must somehow learn to head him off before he manoeuvred himself into a position of power behind her own defences, and perhaps, if it achieved nothing else, her enforced break in the wilds of Northumberland would teach her how to do just that. She fervently hoped so.

Matthew's car, a powerful-looking German model, had been driven round to the Chelsea house while Lucy was in her own flat, packing.

'It's been in the garage under the office-block while I've been unable to drive,' Matthew told her later. 'What do you think? Can you manage it?'

Lucy flicked a quick glance at him, wondering whether he was being sarcastic, but for once he seemed quite serious.

'In my job I've had to get used to coping with all sorts of things, from Land Rovers to battered old heaps that ought to have been in junk yards—and top-of-the-range models like yours. I haven't any worries if you haven't,' she added with a grin. 'You don't mind being driven by someone else—a girl, too? I'd have thought you'd hate it.'

'I don't have much choice, do I?' Matthew remarked drily, which wasn't strictly true, Lucy thought as she went into the kitchen to prepare their meal. He hadn't had to suggest this trip at all—but she wouldn't go into all that again. She'd agreed to go, and she had to make the best of it.

Getting out of London the following morning was more than usually tiresome, and Lucy needed all her concentration to negotiate the hold-ups and diversions, and she dared not so much as glance at the tall figure sitting silently beside her, for fear of reading in his expression the impatience and aggravation she was sure he must be feeling at not being in control of the situation.

When she did finally turn briefly towards him, however, it wasn't disapproval she saw, but a glint of something like admiration in the dark eyes resting on her face.

'As I said yesterday, you're full of surprises, Miss Lucy Ambleside. You handle this car as though you've been driving it for years, and in the most unpromising conditions, too.'

'Thank you, kind sir,' Lucy retorted pertly as she pulled out to overtake a line of heavy lorries, acknowledging the cheeky wave of one of the drivers with a grin. 'And, as I told you, I enjoy driving, especially a car like this.'

With each mile that passed Lucy felt her spirits lift a little higher. Perhaps this trip hadn't been such a bad idea after all. It was a beautiful day, the English countryside looked at its best, the trees just beginning to show a tinge of green—what more could anyone want?

They travelled along in a relaxed silence until, after a while, Matthew's voice broke into Lucy's thoughts.

'We're about halfway, now,' he told her, 'and I always take a break at a café in a village just off the next exit road. It's a bit early for lunch, but they do good coffee and sandwiches.'

'Suits me,' Lucy agreed cheerfully. 'I could do with stretching my legs, I must admit. Just point me in the right direction.'

The café was unremarkable but quiet, and the hot coffee and ham sandwich welcome after the early and difficult start to their journey.

Lucy leaned back gratefully in her chair and cupped her hands around the steaming cup.

'So tell me about this house of yours,' she invited Matthew. 'I don't even know where it is.'

Matthew stared across the room with unfocused eyes, frowning, as though the innocent enquiry had unlocked memories he'd rather have remained dormant.

'It's north of Alnwick, not far from Bamburgh,' he told her slowly after a few moments. 'Stone-built and spacious—rambling, some people might call it. I fell in love with it as soon as I saw it and bought it as a wedding-present for the woman I hoped—then—would be my wife.'

Lucy stared at him, trying not to show her amazement at this sudden revelation. He'd never so much as hinted at the existence of a woman in his life, past or present, and, if the affair had ended unhappily, that explained a lot.

She watched as his mouth tightened and the lines on his face deepened with bitterness. 'She never liked it. As soon as she saw it she told me she wanted nothing to do with it—too cold and bleak, she said, and miles from anywhere. And by "anywhere" she meant shops, hotels, restaurants. . .places where she could have a good time and spend a lot of money. Poor Celia—even the nearest pub is about two or three miles away,' he ended with a harsh laugh.

'Celia?' Lucy enquired softly.

'Celia Trevenn. The world's most acquisitive woman.' A cynical smile touched his lips as Lucy frowned at a sudden picture that slid into her mind. 'I met her once, I think,' she said slowly, 'at a party, a long time ago.'

She might only have met her once, but that was enough to imprint her on to anyone's mind forever. Once seen, never forgotten, that was Celia, Lucy thought with a wry smile. She herself had been standing in a corner just watching the scene when Celia Trevenn had burst in wearing a dress that left little, if anything, to the imagination, and flirting outrageously with every presentable man in sight. She'd swept past Lucy with a quick flick of a glance that had sized her up and simultaneously dismissed her as a competitor for the attention she had been so clearly seeking. Not that Lucy had minded—she'd been more amused than anything, she remembered.

'At a party?' Matthew repeated almost savagely. 'That figures. Parties, nightclubs—all that sort of thing—were, and still are, I'm sure, her life's blood. What I had to offer her just wasn't exciting enough. It was soon after visiting Rookstones that she told me. . .that our affair ended,' he concluded shortly, draining his cup with a swift flick of his wrist.

Lucy looked at his averted face and decided, for both their sakes, that the time had come to change the direction of the conversation, which was hovering on the edge of dangerous territory.

'Rookstones. . .' Lucy savoured the name thoughtfully '. . .I like that.' She stretched out her legs and leaned back in her chair, gazing out into the middle distance as Matthew had done.

'It'll be good to be back in the country for a while,'

she mused. 'London's all very well, but I wouldn't like to spend my life there, not forever.'

The taut lines on Matthew's face eased a fraction as he looked across at her.

'You may find the house a bit bleak, I'm afraid,' he commented. 'It had been allowed to get into a pretty bad state by the former owners, and I'd hoped Celia would enjoy restoring and redecorating it.' The bitterness returned to his voice as he went on, 'But one visit was enough. She never even spent a night there, insisted on moving to a hotel, and told me she never wanted to set foot in the house again. "Bleak House," she called it.'

There were other, crueller things Celia had said, too, but there was no point in resurrecting them again now. Lucy wouldn't want to hear them, and, in any case, they were no concern of hers. They were best left buried.

'But you kept the house—Rookstones,' Lucy observed, interrupting his reverie. 'You didn't think of selling it?'

'Often,' Matthew nodded, 'but I couldn't bring myself to do it. I. . .' he paused, and gave a rueful smile '. . .I like it. It's as simple as that, and I'm always hoping I'll have the time to put it in order. Anyway, you'll see for yourself soon, and maybe even have some ideas yourself of what might be done.'

As they drove through the flaking iron gates Lucy felt a flash of fellow-feeling for Celia, whose heart must have sunk to her elegant boots at her first sight of the rambling grey stone house protected by an almost threatening ring of huge elms full of the rooks that gave the house its name.

Bushes and shrubs, overgrown through neglect, crowded in round the building and added to the general air of decayed dilapidation, and for a moment Lucy, too, felt she wanted to turn round and drive to somewhere warm and welcoming, but she felt Matthew's eyes on her, waiting to pick up her slightest reaction, so she suppressed an instinctive sigh and smiled gently at him.

'I suppose I have to admit that at first sight it does look a bit—well, uncared for,' she ventured as tactfully as she could. 'Specially if you weren't prepared. But if those shrubs were cut back a bit, and you could get a proper look at the house. . .' She paused, scrutinising the building. 'Even now you can see it has lovely proportions.'

The muscles of Matthew's face relaxed a fraction, but he said nothing as he climbed rather stiffly out of the car and stood looking round as though seeing it for the first time through someone else's eyes.

'I suppose——' he began, then shook his head. 'Come on, let's go inside.'

He reached out impulsively and caught at Lucy's hand, then froze, as though realising what he'd done, and released it at once, turning away to walk quickly away down the path.

'Don't worry,' he called back tersely over his shoulder. 'Everything *indoors* should be clean and ready for us—and warm, too. There's a woman from the village, Mrs Weston, who has the key and keeps the place aired and tidy. I told her we were coming. She should be here, waiting for us.'

Lucy followed Matthew's tall figure round the side of the house to what was presumably the back door, wondering why he had reacted so quickly to that instinctive gesture. It was natural, after all, that he should want to share his enthusiasm with her, especially after his experience with Celia. Why shouldn't he reach out to her physically? There was nothing wrong in that, unless. . .

Lucy's heart turned over in alarm. He couldn't, surely, be beginning to feel something, some attraction, for her? *That* wasn't why he'd wanted to bring her up here to this lonely place? Had she been appallingly naïve in agreeing to come here with him, too caught up in her own anxieties to see what might be behind this apparently sudden and only too plausible change of plan?

The broad back in front of her gave nothing away, but as Lucy followed him she recalled other occasions which could—should—have given her pause for thought; the odd glint in his eyes, an unfinished phrase that seemed to leave its meaning hanging in the air, and not for the first time she told herself she *must* remain on her guard.

Take care, a small voice whispered to her. This man would be ruthless if he decided you were what he wanted. Remember the scorpion's deadly sting.

A shiver shook Lucy's slight frame as Matthew swung round to face her.

'You're cold,' he remarked. 'Come on, into the house. Mrs Weston will have lit a fire, I expect.'

He strode off then, calling Mrs Weston's name, and leaving Lucy to make her own way in, wondering now whether she hadn't been over-reacting to that gesture of Matthew's. He hadn't *held* her hand, but dropped it as soon as he'd realised what he'd done, but even so, she must remain watchful, just in case. . .

Matthew had left her in a sort of stone-flagged lobby, the sort of place you'd expect, in a more lived-in house, to find old coats, umbrellas, wellington boots and baskets full of drying bulbs—all the outdoor clutter of a country family. But here there was barely anything to show the house was ever inhabited. . .Well, Matthew had warned her it would be bleak. She'd better go and discover the worst.

'Oh, this is *nice*!' Lucy burst out involuntarily as she went through the inner door and found herself standing in a huge, old-fashioned kitchen.

She stared round, open-mouthed, then turned to

Matthew, who was standing by another doorway watching her with amusement.

'This is extraordinary,' Lucy told him. 'The whole room ought to be transported to a museum. Nothing can have been touched since the house was built!'

Then another, more worrying thought struck her.

'That range,' she ventured hesitatingly, as though fearful of the answer. 'Is that what I'll be expected to cook on?'

'Bless you, no!'

A small wiry woman with bird-bright eyes bustled out from where she had been hidden behind Matthew.

'Oh, I'm sorry,' Matthew said. 'This is Mrs Weston, Lucy. Mrs Weston, this is Miss Lucy Ambleside, my housekeeper.'

'Just a temporary measure,' Lucy put in quickly, anxious to allay any possible misunderstandings about her relationship with Matthew. 'Just until Mrs Portland comes back from Australia. And part-time chauffeuse,' she added with a grin.

Mrs Weston nodded. The explanation seemed to satisfy her, and her ready acceptance of it helped ease any lingering doubts Lucy might have had about Matthew. He clearly had no reputation up here as a philanderer. She would be as safe in Rookstones as she had been in London.

'Perhaps you'd like to give Miss Ambleside a guided tour of the house, and show her where she'll be sleeping?' Matthew suggested. 'My leg's a bit stiff still after sitting in the car. I'll stay downstairs for the moment.'

'Do call me Lucy,' Lucy told Mrs Weston as the older woman led the way out into the hall after putting her mind at rest about the cooking arrangements. There was a scullery leading off the kitchen, complete with modern cooker, washing-machine and drier, and even a dishwasher, all brand new and hardly ever used, by the look of them.

'Right you are, pet,' Mrs Weston said cheerfully. 'And my name's Dorothy, but most people call me Dot. Now, where shall we begin?'

The house was, as Matthew had said, big and rambling with little unexpected stairways and passages leading to back-bedrooms and attics, mostly unused, and again Lucy felt a wave of sympathy for Celia as she noted the shabby wallpaper and worn carpets. How that smart, ultra-modern lady's heart must have sunk at the prospect of having to renovate all this, and yet, given time and a lot of money, and above all an imaginative designer, the house could be made into something pretty amazing, Lucy thought, gazing round the bedroom Dot Weston had chosen for her.

This room, for instance, cried out for light paint, and flowered wallpaper and curtains to cover up the brownish walls and shiny green rayon at the windows. The bed, which appeared comfortable enough when Lucy sat on it, was covered with a faded pink quilt, and the furniture was a nondescript assortment dating back to the 1920s, Lucy guessed.

Dot watched her expression and grinned.

'It's all clean, love, I've seen to that myself, but I do agree—there's a lot needs doing here.'

She sat companionably beside Lucy on the bed. 'I think Mr Fenn thought that other lady would see to it all, give the place a thorough going-over, but it wasn't to be, poor man.'

She paused a moment, then put her hand over Lucy's, her eyes twinkling. 'I do have to confess, pet, when I saw you downstairs with Mr Fenn, I thought he'd found himself another young lady. That other one wasn't suitable, you could see that, but you——'

'No chance,' Lucy interrupted her firmly. 'We argue too much, for one thing, and our relationship is purely a business one.'

Dot Weston sighed and stood up to consider Lucy, her head on one side, making her look more bird-like than ever.

'That's a pity, pet. I reckon you're just what he needs—someone calm and sympathetic. Someone to make a real home for him.'

Her sharp eyes narrowed as she peered more closely into Lucy's. 'I bet you're Pisces,' she said knowingly. 'Am I right?'

Lucy's eyes widened as she stared back in surprise. 'Yes, you are, as a matter of fact. But how——?'

Dot folded her arms and nodded her satisfaction. 'Thought so. You've got the look. . .something about your eyes, sea-green—North Sea, that is, nothing to do with the Mediterranean—and that quiet way you have with you. You'll like it here, I know, more than that other one. . .what was her name?'

'Celia,' Lucy told her. 'Celia Trevenn.'

'Hmm.' Dot pursed her lips. 'Never took to her, not that she gave me long to try. But you. . .'

Their eyes met in instinctive liking to one another, and Dot grinned. 'Never mind me, love. My Ron tells me I'm touched. Now, you settle in here and come down when you're ready. I've got a salad all ready, and some home-made soup to start with.'

She paused in the doorway and added softly, 'Whatever it is you're looking for, you'll likely find it here.'

Lucy stared after her, then smiled, wondering whether she might not be right. Not that she was looking for anything in particular, only peace and quiet, and she might indeed find that in this remote spot. Already she sensed a burden beginning to ease from her mind and she felt more content than she had been for weeks, and she'd only been in the place less than an hour.

Perhaps she would have cause to be grateful to Matthew, after all. . .

Matthew, too, seemed to have shed some of his London stress, Lucy thought, as she met him in the drawing-room, staring out of the window at the overgrown garden. His shoulders were relaxed and his hands weren't clenched, as she had so often seen them, but linked easily behind his back.

Dot's words came into her mind, to be rapidly dismissed. 'You're just what he needs. . .'

Silly woman, Lucy thought, but not crossly. Now *there* was a case of someone letting her imagination run away with her. Matthew didn't need anyone. If anyone was perfectly self-sufficient, he was that man.

Matthew remained in a relaxed frame of mind all through lunch as he chatted easily to Lucy about the house and his plans for it, and described some of the landmarks of the surrounding area.

'And the sea?' Lucy ventured. 'Is that far?'

'The sea?' Matthew echoed in surprise. 'No, only a mile or two—as the rook flies. Why? You're not thinking of taking a swim, are you? That'd be the easiest way to catch pneumonia I know.'

Lucy laughed. 'No, don't worry. I'm not a complete masochist! It's just that. . .' Her voice trailed away and her eyes travelled to the window to stare out at the rooks wheeling over the elms.

'Yes?' Matthew prompted her.

'The sea is something special,' she heard herself telling him, with an ironic smile at her own expense. 'My natural element, I suppose, being a Pisces.'

Then her face grew more serious as she went on, 'The shifting colours. . .all that restless movement, and the power of the waves. . . I just find it all fascinating, and comforting, too, in a strange way. So strong and impersonal. It's been like that since time began, and puts all our petty problems into perspective, somehow.'

'Hmm,' Matthew murmured doubtfully, studying her

almost wistful expression. 'I'd never thought of it quite like that, I must confess. My interest in the sea is more practical—geared to what use I can make of it. Windsurfing, sailing—all that. And I can't do any of those things just now, can I?'

His mouth clamped shut and his eyes flashed a brief warning before he spoke again.

'We could go and look at it this afternoon, if you like? We mustn't keep you from your natural element any longer than we need.'

The words were mocking but the tone of his voice less abrasive than Lucy was used to hearing it, and she smiled back at him.

'Tomorrow will do,' she told him. 'I think I've done enough driving for one day, and it would be nice to spend today settling in and getting to know the house. Oh—and I must dash off a note to Bella. Someone ought to know where I am, and I could ask Dot to post it on her way home.'

'Why not ring?' Matthew asked reasonably as he stretched behind him for the bowl of fruit on the sideboard.

Lucy grinned, thinking of all the inevitable explanations, even recriminations and warnings, a telephone call would entail.

'Writing's simpler,' she said. 'Bella would want all the whys and wherefores——'

'—And no doubt add dire warnings about the folly of coming up here to the back of beyond with a tall, dark stranger,' Matthew added casually. 'There's no saying what dangers could befall you, so far from civilisation.'

'Like pneumonia?' Lucy suggested, her pulses accelerating unaccountably.

'That wasn't quite what I had in mind, nor would it be what your friend feared, either,' Matthew murmured as he concentrated on a neat dissection of an apple.

Lucy pretended not to have heard him as she watched him from beneath lowered lids, and for the first time she found herself wondering what difference it might have made if they had met in other circumstances.

Supposing he had come to Bella's party and she had been introduced to him socially? Then they could have chosen whether to have got to know one another better, instead of being thrust into one another's reluctant company.

This unexpected trip would give them the opportunity to do just that, if they wanted to take it. . .but did she want to? Wasn't it to escape problems connected with relationships of any sort that she'd wanted to get away from London? And the last thing she wanted was to jump from the proverbial frying-pan into another fire.

'So you'd better write that note,' Matthew's voice interrupted her uncomfortable thoughts. 'I'm not sure when Mrs Weston's bus goes, but I know it's early in the afternoon, and she won't want to miss it. It's the only one.'

And then I'll be quite alone here, with Matthew, in this strange house, Lucy thought with a spurt of alarm as she went in search of something to write to Bella on. Then she pulled herself together. If he hadn't tried anything on in London, why should he start now?

'I'll see you in a couple of days, ' Dot told Lucy as they went out to the front gate together. 'You won't need me every day, but this is a big place to look after on your own, and I expect you could do with some extra help.'

'And the company,' Lucy told her.

'Company?' Dot sounded surprised, then grinned. 'If you say so, pet.'

She opened her mouth as though to say something else, but thought better of it as she turned to wave cheerily back at Lucy. 'See you soon, then, love. Bye for now.'

Lucy wandered back into the garden. There was no sign of Matthew, who had disappeared upstairs after lunch, presumably to unpack, so now she would do all the exploring she wanted on her own.

If Matthew really wanted her opinion on restoring Rookstones to its former state—whatever that had been—she thought crossly as she fought her way round the overgrown paths, the first thing she'd recommend would be the services of a good landscape gardener, or at the least a tree surgeon.

Goodness only knew when had been the last time anyone had done any work in the poor garden, which once upon a time must have been well planned and cared for, judging from the shrubs she was able to recognise beneath the wild sycamores and elders sprouting everywhere.

And there had been a kitchen garden too, now completely overtaken by a forest of grass and thistles. Good for wildlife, no doubt, but rather a waste.

Still, if Matthew never intended to live here, the birds and insects might as well keep it to themselves, Lucy thought, watching a pair of blackbirds eyeing her warily from a hawthorn bush growing in what must have been a strawberry-bed.

It was strange that Matthew had kept the house at all after Celia had left him. You'd have thought he'd have wanted to get rid of it, or at the very least developed its potential as a holiday let.

Lucy was now at the back of the house, and found herself passing a shallow flight of stone steps leading up to some french windows belonging to a room she hadn't yet seen from the inside.

Curious, she climbed up and peered inside, and what

she saw made her catch her breath in delight and disbelief.

It couldn't be, not here, in this poor neglected house—not a grand piano!

Lucy stared at it in utter astonishment for a second or two, almost expecting it to vanish as a figment of her imagination, but it seemed solid enough.

Then she almost ran round to the back door, pushing her way impatiently through the overhanging branches, not even noticing when a thorn from a rampant climbing rose scratched her cheek, drawing drops of blood. A piano! she kept saying to herself, and not any old upright, either, but a full concert grand.

It couldn't be in working order, though. That simply wasn't possible.

Lucy hurried through the house, opening each door in turn until she came to the very last one at the end of the passage at the opposite end to the kitchen, and there it was, in all its glory, dusted and polished and waiting for someone to play it.

Almost holding her breath in anticipation, Lucy found herself tiptoeing across the large, empty room, then lifting the lid to reveal the maker's name—Bechstein!

Whatever was it doing here in this dilapidated old house, a magnificent instrument like this?

Lucy stared down at the yellowing keys and stretched out her hand to caress them, closing her eyes to conjure up the sound this aristocrat must have made in its heyday.

'You've found it, then?'

Lucy whirled round, the sudden movement making her fingers press the keys she hadn't dared play, and a deeply resonant chord rang out round the room.

'It's in tune!' she gasped, gazing wide-eyed at Matthew, who stood in the doorway watching her with interest. 'Whatever is it doing here?'

'It belonged to the last owners,' Matthew told her. 'They got it for their son, who was a professional musician, but he decided it wasn't right for him, and when I bought the house I bought the Bechstein as well. Celia had said she wanted to learn—just a fad, of course,' he said bitterly, 'but it seemed a pity to let it go. . . And it's a good investment, too,' he added with a mocking lift of his eyebrow at Lucy's outraged expression.

He came into the room and laid a hand on the gleaming wood. 'Actually, I was thinking I ought to sell it. It ought to be used, not left here, but now. . .well, we'll have to see.'

His eyes narrowed as he stared closely at her, his hands thrust deep into his pockets.

'*You* play, don't you? The way you looked at the piano——' he nodded towards it '—you had real love in your eyes. Why didn't you mention it before?'

Lucy smiled wryly. 'I only play for myself. I can't explain, but somehow I find it a release.'

'Like the sea,' Matthew murmured.

'Maybe.' Lucy frowned. 'I find it difficult to talk about, and I don't usually tell people because once they know I can play they're always wanting me to "give them a tune".'

'What's wrong with that?' Matthew asked her.

'Nothing in principle, but more often than not they don't really want to listen. It's just background noise to most of them, something to talk against. It makes me so angry!'

Lucy moved away to go and stand by the french windows, her hands clenched fiercely by her sides.

'That's two things I didn't know about you, Lucy Ambleside, that I've learned since we've been here. You're a very secretive person, aren't you? Your feelings run deep, like the sea.'

Matthew's voice was soft, and there was no hint of

mockery in it, but Lucy was so wrapped up in her own thoughts that she hadn't heard him move across the room, and she looked round now to find him standing close beside her, his eyes dark and unfathomable, yet with a gleam in their depths that held her gaze locked into his while the silence settled round them.

'You play whenever you like,' Matthew said quietly. 'I won't disturb you, I promise, and there's all the music you could want in the cabinet over there.'

'Thanks.'

Lucy turned to walk over to the walnut cupboard against the far wall, but Matthew stopped her, reaching out to grasp her arm.

'You've scratched yourself,' he observed, touching her cheek gently with his finger, and his lips curved into a smile. 'And your hair's got bits of twig in it. Do you know, I believe that's the first time I've seen you looking untidy? It's quite a relief to know you can.'

His fingers felt warm as they lingered on the smoothness of her skin and, for a wild moment, as Lucy wondered whether the casual caress might be about to turn into something more significant, she felt a sudden lurch in the pit of her stomach—the surging, unmistakable ache of desire.

Aghast, she managed a shaky laugh. 'I must go and do something about that, then. And thanks for the offer about the piano. I might take you up on it if my duties leave me time.'

Then, trying not to show how desperate she was to escape his following gaze, she walked quickly away, her steps turning into a run as she headed upstairs to the relative safety of her own room.

CHAPTER SIX

LUCY closed the door behind her and leaned against it for a moment to get her breath back. Her pulses were still racing, and not just from the dash upstairs.

Almost as though of their own volition, her fingers strayed to the scratch on her cheek which other fingers had touched with the caress that had stirred up such a turmoil within her. Had Matthew noticed anything? she wondered desperately, for that was the very last thing she would have wanted.

Anxiously she peered at her reflection in the mirror for the slightest tell-tale hint of what she was feeling. Would he have put that flush on her cheeks down to her excitement over the piano, or would he have guessed the real reason behind her unnaturally heightened colour and the brightness in her eye?

One thing was certain. She must at all costs keep herself as far removed from Matthew as was possible in the circumstances in which she'd found herself. At least now she'd had warning of the extent of her vulnerability, and she must protect it every minute they were together. It might not be easy, but it was essential for her own peace of mind.

With rigorous self-control Lucy forced her thoughts away from the man who had aroused such an unexpected and unwelcome response in her senses, not even daring to ask herself how or why he had managed to wreak such havoc with her emotions. The implications were just too dangerous to contemplate.

Instead, she busied herself with her unpacking, spending perhaps longer over putting all her things away than she might otherwise have done, to avoid running the risk of coming face to face with Matthew for as long as possible.

Then she explored the rest of the house, ending up back in the kitchen, where she investigated the stores situation.

Dot had got in all the essentials and some lamb chops to cook for this evening's meal. Tomorrow she must go shopping *and* try to discover how long Matthew was intending to stay up here.

He's promised to take her on a tour round the area, too, hadn't he?

Lucy put the kettle on to make a pot of tea, and stared at the pattern on the cup she was holding. Driving round together would force them into close proximity again, wouldn't it? Inevitably they would touch one another. . .

Pull yourself together, girl, she chided herself sternly, as she put the cups on to the only tray she could find, a battered old tin one that should have been put out for jumble years ago. He's touched you before, even held your arm, and you didn't go into these Victorian vapours then.

No, a little voice whispered, but you did feel *something*. Be honest. Remember the warmth of his hand on your arm when he took you back to your flat? Those moments he held your hand, and. . .

'Stop it!' Lucy silenced the voice sharply, rubbing her arm as though to rid it of any lingering trace of his touch, then picked up the tray and marched resolutely through to the living-room.

Matthew made no reference, even implicitly, to the episode that had disturbed Lucy so much, nor to the scratch which still scarred her cheek, and the rest of the day passed sedately enough. After supper Lucy excused herself from accepting Matthew's invitation to come and sit with him in the drawing-room.

'It's been a long day, what with the early start and everything. I think I'll turn in for an early night,' she told him.

Matthew looked up from the book he was reading and smiled.

'If you're sure? I want you to think of Rookstones as your home while we're here.'

Lucy nodded. 'Thanks, but I am rather tired.'

'Sleep well, then, and I hope you'll be comfortable up there.'

Lucy did in fact sleep like a log, only waking with a jerk when a gust of wind rattled the frame of her window some time after eight o'clock.

'Goodness!' She stretched luxuriously and hoped Matthew hadn't wanted to make an early start, but she couldn't hear any sound that indicated he was already up. Probably he'd been as tired as she had been.

She lay in bed for a while letting her thoughts drift, though keeping them firmly from yesterday's episode in the music-room, and listening to the wind which had got up in the night. The weather had turned very stormy, by the sound of it, and bitterly cold. A chill grey light seeped in through the drawn curtains, and in her mind's eye Lucy could see the sea, just a few miles away, the waves angrily white-topped as they tore up the beach like wild creatures in search of their prey.

Strange, the fascination the sea had for her, in any of its moods. Of course, it couldn't really have anything to do with her star sign, that was just people's fancy, but there were grains of truth in how Nick — and Dot, too — had described her, without either of them knowing her very well.

Lucy smiled. She must remember to ask Dot about Scorpios, and see if her assessment tallied with Nick's, she thought as at last, and with great reluctance, she climbed out of her warm bed and shivered in the freezing room. No central heating here yet—another good reason for Celia to take against the house.

As she pulled on her warmest clothes, her mind went back to Nick, wondering where he was now. His teeth wouldn't be chattering with cold, that was for sure, as he dressed beneath his beloved desert sky. It was strange that, attractive as he was, when *he* had kissed her on the same cheek that Matthew had touched, nothing had happened at all to disturb the equilibrium of her senses, whereas it had taken only one caress. . .

No, don't even think of it, Lucy told herself again. Breakfast, that's what you must concentrate on. Breakfast, housework, shopping. Keep your mind on one thing at a time, and put that particular episode behind you.

Matthew had decided to test out his leg by driving, so Lucy was able to seat herself so as to keep as far away from him as possible without it looking too obvious what she was doing. Even in the pub, where they had lunch after she had done her shopping, Lucy managed to choose a table where she could sit opposite him, rather than on one of the cosy, thigh-touching benches against the wall.

In any case, Matthew was so pleased at being back in the driving-seat—literally—that he hardly seemed to notice her presence beside him, she decided, glancing across at his rapt profile as they headed towards the coast.

'You've never been to this part of the country before?' he asked as they drove through a small place called Seahouses.

Lucy shook her head. 'No, somehow I've never needed to, in my job, and holidays always seemed to take me in other directions. Warmer ones,' she added with a shiver as she noted the grasses on the dunes blown almost horizontal by the gale.

'It was you who wanted to see the sea,' Matthew pointed out, 'and we're here now, so you can't chicken out, not when I've brought you here specially. Come on. Out you get.'

He had parked on a grass verge by the sand-hills, and Lucy steeled herself to take the hand he offered to help her out of the car, feeling the strength in the fingers grasping hers and their warmth—but nothing else. Not even a tremor touched her heart, and Lucy had no time to do more than merely register this interesting fact as she needed all her concentration to keep her balance in the gale that buffeted around her, almost knocking her off her feet.

Matthew scarcely paused to see if she was following him, but set off at a brisk pace up through the dunes.

Lucy almost had to run to keep up with his long strides, stumbling in the soft sand and fighting against the wind, which was blowing in so hard straight off the sea that it was difficult to make any headway.

'Nearly there,' Matthew called out when he was almost at the top. 'Come on, Lucy. There it is—look! Is that bracing enough for you?'

Panting and flushed from her exertions, Lucy reached his side on the crest of the dunes and stared out in front of her.

The tide was coming in, and the breakers roared up the beach, driven in by the wind which whipped up their foaming crests so that as far as the eye could see there were white horses plunging and rearing in dizzying profusion.

Lucy turned to Matthew, her eyes shining.

'Isn't that fantastic?' She almost had to shout to make her voice heard against the tumult of the elements. 'Come on, let's go down on to the sand.'

Just to her right there was a path leading down to the shore, and Lucy clambered down it, stumbling in her haste, then, reaching level ground, she ran to the water's edge, her hair streaming out behind her.

The noise down here was even more deafening as the waves crashed down in endless succession, seeming to devour one another in their urge to take possession of the land, and the wind...

Lucy felt herself swaying as the gale tore at her clothes, howling with rage as she fought to keep upright. Stretching out her arms to help her keep her balance, she found herself laughing out loud with pure joy at this spectacle of unleashed power.

She ran along the beach, dancing on the edge of the water-line, taunting the waves to reach her as they encroached ever further inland, and she stooped every now and again to pick up a pebble which she hurled into the sea as far as she could against the force of the wind which still roared round her, blotting out every other sound and drumming into her head so that she became oblivious to everything but the raging of the elements and her own exhilaration.

She bent to pick up a shell gleaming on the wet sand, momentarily unaware of the slight lull in the tumult around her as the sea drew in its breath to allow a breaker, more enormous than any of its companions, to rear up, uncurling its foaming head almost lazily before crashing down to come tearing up the sand towards her, intent on dragging her away into its depths.

'Lucy! Watch out!'

Matthew's shout at full volume was only just audible over the clamour, and Lucy swung round in the nick of time to see the monstrous wave heading straight for her.

Running back, she tripped and almost fell, but two arms, strong and powerful, seized her and almost carried her back up the beach to safer ground in the comparative shelter of the dunes.

'That wasn't very sensible, Miss Ambleside,' Matthew

observed drily as Lucy, laughing and gasping, fought to get her breath back. 'I thought for one minute I was in danger of losing my housekeeper for good. And that would be a great pity.'

His voice dropped and the arm, which Lucy suddenly realised was still round her waist, tightened its hold, making her look quickly up into Matthew's face. Now it wasn't her narrow escape from a watery fate which made her breath come so unevenly, but an expression in the dark, glinting eyes she had never seen there before.

She had scarcely had time to register its appearance, let alone begin to analyse it, as, without any warning, Matthew bent to kiss her, touching her mouth gently with his before drawing back slowly as though to assess her response.

The fingers of his free hand strayed to the scratch on her cheek, then moved to cup her chin, tilting her face back so that he could search deep into her eyes. Then his brows drew into a heavy bar.

'I'm sorry,' he said abruptly, releasing her. He turned away, so that Lucy could only see the back of his head, and something about the proudly rigid set of his shoulders made her heart lurch within her breast, and again she felt that surge of emotion rush through her like one of the waves out there on the sea's edge, as powerful and as overwhelming.

'Matthew,' she said softly, her pulses racing so fast her voice sounded shaky even to her own ears. 'Why did you turn away?'

Matthew moved slowly round to face her, but made no attempt to touch her.

'I thought,' he began, then shook his head in disbelief in what he read in her eyes. 'Yesterday, when I touched your cheek. . .' He reached out and rested his fingers once again on her face. 'You ran away, and I thought, just now, the message was the same.'

Lucy raised her own hand and covered his fingers with hers in a gesture of acceptance.

'I was frightened,' she said in a low voice which Matthew had to come close to hear, 'but not of you.' Her eyes were wide, and as luminous as the sea. 'I was scared of what I felt—it was all so sudden and unexpected, and I wasn't sure I wanted even to admit those feelings to myself.'

'And now?' Matthew's voice was harsh as he tensed himself for her reply.

Lucy's lips curved into a tremulous smile. 'Now I know they're too strong for me,' she said simply, and her hand dropped to her side as she waited for Matthew's response.

He caught his breath and moved even closer to her, then hesitated. 'You still haven't told me whether those strong feelings are ones you welcome. Whether they match the ones raging inside *me*.'

A sudden gust of wind reached for Lucy's hair, teasing it into strands that whipped round her face, and Matthew brushed them aside as he searched her face.

'Oh, yes,' she whispered at last. 'I welcome them.'

Then, with a cry of exultation that broke into the howl of the gale, Matthew pulled her against him, crushing her slender frame against his powerful body with a strength as merciless as that of the elements themselves.

Lucy felt warm fingers touch her chin and she lifted her face, rejoicing in the assault of his mouth, which bruised hers in a long and passionate kiss that left her struggling for breath.

'I've wanted to do this for so long,' Matthew told her in a strangely hoarse voice when at last he released her. 'Sometimes I didn't know how I could hold back any longer, and if you'd really left me. . .'

Again his arms went round her, his body hard and

demanding as his hands pressed her to him before moving to lie against her breast.

With a little shudder Lucy reached up to the back of his neck, running her hand through the thick dark hair to bring his head down to hers once more, offering her mouth to his.

'It's no use here,' Matthew murmured against her hair, and Lucy thought she heard something like a chuckle.

'These jackets are fine for keeping the weather out—but they are only too successful in keeping out everything else as well. Dammit, Lucy, I want to touch *you*, not this armour-plating!'

Both he and Lucy were wearing stiff, unyielding waxed jackets to protect themselves against the onslaught of the weather, and Lucy looked down at her firmly encased body with a quiver of apprehension.

'Perhaps you feel safer with it on?'

Everything had happened so quickly that Lucy no longer knew what she felt or how she ought to respond, either to Matthew or to her own tumultuous emotions. She stared up at him helplessly.

Matthew seemed to sense something of her confusion, for his face softened suddenly. He stepped back a pace and took her cold hand in his, holding it for an instant before tucking it away in his pocket.

'Come on. Let's go back to the car,' he invited her. 'It's far too cold to go on standing here, and, besides, we've things to sort out.'

He smiled gently down at her, then, side by side, and with Lucy's hand still in Matthew's firm possession, they retraced their steps through the dunes.

Matthew opened the passenger-door of his car and waited till Lucy was safely inside before climbing in beside her, turning slightly to face her and resting his arm along the back of her seat, but making no attempt to renew the embrace or even to touch her, for which Lucy was grateful.

The deep-set eyes beneath the heavy brows studied her intently, narrowing as they tried to penetrate into the thoughts whirling behind Lucy's clear gaze.

'Maybe I went too quickly,' Matthew said in a low voice, 'but holding you, at last, I couldn't stop myself. And you let me kiss you, Lucy. And those things you said. . .'

He didn't finish, and Lucy nodded slowly, too honest to pretend even to herself that she hadn't welcomed his embrace or offered her lips willingly for that second, passionate kiss. Nor was she so naïve that she didn't know that that kiss could so easily have been a prelude to something much, much more—a commitment, even, for she suspected Matthew was not the sort of man to indulge in casual affairs.

Was that what lay at the back of this hesitation—a fear that he might demand more than she was ready to give?

She stared down at her hands lying in her lap. 'I don't seem to be sure of anything any more,' she said in hardly more than a whisper. 'Back there——' she waved vaguely in the direction of the beach '——I did want you to kiss me, I can't pretend I didn't. But then. . .oh, I don't know, maybe I panicked. But I need time to be sure—please, Matthew? There's been someone else, you see, until not very long ago, and I don't know whether I'm ready for——'

'For something like this?'

The arm which had been lying along the back of her seat moved gently to turn her towards him, holding her in a light but possessive grip.

Powerless to resist, Lucy felt her heart begin to pound furiously as Matthew's other hand moved to the zip of her jacket, sliding it with infinite and tantalising slowness to her waist while his dark eyes held hers in unwavering thrall.

She swayed towards him as his arms tightened round her and his lips came down at last on hers as they had done back on the beach, hard and predatory, crushing her mouth mercilessly.

A gasp escaped her as Matthew's hand slipped inside her jacket and began caressing her body, roving over her back and her shoulders till she felt his fingers linger warm and dry against the soft skin of her neck.

Lucy clung to him, not daring to lift her head from its resting-place against his chest for fear of what he might read in her eyes, but her resistance was of little avail.

'Look at me,' Matthew commanded her softly in a voice husky with longing, and then, when Lucy still hesitated, his hand raised her chin just enough for him to be able to look into her face, and whatever it was he saw was enough.

'I knew it,' he said, enfolding her again closely in his arms with a little laugh of triumph. 'You do feel something for me, don't you? Just let it happen, Lucy. Don't fight it.'

He kissed her again, more gently this time, his lips brushing against hers in a caress so sensual that Lucy had to summon up all her strength to prevent herself from capitulating to him utterly.

He thrust his hand inside her coat once more to explore every contour and softness of her body until, at last, with an almost convulsive movement, it came to rest on the gentle curve of her breast, which swelled to his touch as he cupped it in his warm palm.

With a little cry she couldn't silence Lucy wound her own arms round his neck, pressing his head to hers as now it was her lips that sought his in an anguished and passionate response, but even as her back arched towards him again she heard that voice inside her, fainter now than when she'd heard it before, but insistent, none the less.

Wait, something was telling her. You don't know this man. Remember that ruthless aggression you've seen in action so often. You give in to him now, and he'll never let you go. And you can't be sure you want that. Not now. Not yet.

But the hand that was holding her, caressing her so sensuously, wasn't aggressive, Lucy argued in silent desperation. It was as tender as the light in the dark eyes resting on her face, eyes black and fathomless as mountain pools in which she could lose herself and drown. . .

'Even now you're holding something back from me, aren't you?' Matthew murmured softly against her hair. 'I can see it in your eyes. There's a shadow there, like a shadow on the sea.'

He kissed them with such gentleness that Lucy felt herself melting again into his arms, and, as his mouth moved to her lips, her neck, her throat, his hand slipped under her sweater to find the naked softness beneath, stroking the smooth skin of her midriff. . .travelling up to find the fullness of her breasts. . .

'But you mustn't be anxious,' she heard him say, as though from a great distance. 'There's no need, no need at all.'

Now his hand began to slide, almost imperceptibly, to the top of her jeans, and Lucy gave a kind of shudder and struggled upright, seizing his hands and pushing them away in a fever of desperation.

'No, Matthew—you mustn't. . . I can't. . .Please, give me time. I didn't know, you see, how you felt, and we don't really know one another yet, not enough. . .' Her voice trailed away into a helpless silence.

'Why do you think I wanted us to come to Northumberland?' Matthew asked at last.

Lucy stared at him, wide-eyed with suspicion. 'What

do you mean? You wanted to check over the house, didn't you?'

Matthew laughed drily. 'That too, but it was hardly urgent. No——' He withdrew his arm from her shoulders and picked up her hand to play idly with her fingers. 'I knew if I told you the real reason, you'd never have agreed to come, so——'

'So you pretended you needed me to drive, *and* insisted on my sticking to my contract?'

Matthew nodded, his infuriating eyebrow lifting ironically as he watched her take in the whole implication of his scheming.

'So you could have your wicked way with me?' she asked in a voice not quite steady as she attempted a not very convincing joke.

Matthew's eyes narrowed. 'You may not know me very well, but I hope you don't think as badly of me as that.'

Lucy flushed. 'No. No, I don't. I'm sorry.' She paused, head bowed, before going on. 'So why *did* you want me to come here?'

'Would you believe me if I said it was so we could get to know one another better, away from London and all that's been on your mind these last few days? And then, I thought, maybe, if you began to understand how I felt. . .?'

Matthew didn't have to finish. His meaning was only too clear.

'So isn't it about time you told me just what—or who — it is who's hurt you?' he went on in a different, almost harsh voice. 'And what it was they did to upset you so much? It might even help, you never know.'

'Oh, no—that is. . .Look, don't you think we'd better be getting back?' Lucy asked in mounting agitation. Explaining to Matthew about Stephen was something she couldn't face, or at least not now, when her emotions were already seething. 'I've all the shopping still to put away, and some of it's frozen,' she added, grasping at this lifeline. 'It'll be thawed out if we don't get it into the freezer. And then there's supper to prepare...'

Matthew stared at her in disbelief, then broke into a laugh. 'Oh, Lucy, you're marvellous! But I won't let you off the hook so easily, you know that. We've come so far, I'm not going to allow you to escape. I know you want me, and when that shadow in your eyes has disappeared...'

He leaned across and kissed her lightly, then, without another word, switched the car engine on, slipped it into gear and headed for home.

'As for getting things ready for supper,' Matthew commented when they were driving in through the gates, as though continuing their previous conversation without a break, 'that's no problem. We'll go out somewhere. There are a couple of nice pubs quiet enough to be able to talk in.'

He rested one hand on her knee as a tacit reminder to Lucy of what he'd said about not allowing her to escape. It wasn't a comfortable thought, but maybe she did owe him an explanation of some sort, however painful it would be not only to her—as she relived times and events she was trying to forget—but to Matthew, too, as inevitably any mention of broken engagements would remind him of his own.

Remembering the glimpses she'd had of his pent-up anger whenever Celia had been mentioned, Lucy flinched mentally at the prospect of seeing it unleashed, and wondered whether she couldn't head off his insistent curiosity about her past; but dropping subjects wasn't in Matthew's Scorpio nature, she should have learnt that much by now, and, sure enough, no sooner had he settled her at a secluded table in the corner of the pub dining-room that evening, than he raised the question she had been dreading.

'Weren't you going to tell me why you've been so anxious these past few days, Lucy? I'm a good listener—and you can't hide away up here forever.'

Lucy's pale cheeks flushed. 'What do you mean?' she asked, although she knew perfectly well what lay behind those words.

'You're not going to try to pretend you didn't agree to come up here with me to get away from something—or someone—in particular? You can be as devious as you think I am when it suits you, can't you?'

Matthew raised his wine glass to his lips and perused her intently over the rim, his eyes black in the restaurant's subdued light. Lucy forced herself to meet them, with an embarrassed smile.

'I'm sorry. Was it so obvious?' She sighed. 'I sometimes think. . .' Her voice drifted off into silence, but Matthew leaned forwards across the table.

'Yes? You think what?'

Lucy lifted her hands helplessly, knowing she might as well tell him what had gone through her mind as lay herself open to his persistent probing.

'Just that you seem to have a knack—gift. . .' she shrugged '. . .some intuition, anyway, that tells you what I'm thinking even before I know it myself. It's very unsettling.'

Matthew grinned suddenly. 'Good,' he said smugly. 'I like unsettling you. You always appear so calm and efficient—self-sufficient, even—that I get a perverse pleasure in taking you by surprise.'

He reached out for one of Lucy's hands and turned it over, then bent quickly to place a kiss on the palm.

'So won't you tell me what's on your mind?' he asked in a low, almost pleading voice. 'There's someone—a man,' he added more harshly, 'who means something to you. Isn't that why you held back from giving yourself up to your real feelings for me, when we were in the car? Because you did want me, didn't you?'

There was a glint in his eyes that held hers. As yet it was still only a pale reflection of the fire smouldering within him, but a word from her and that fire would be ignited into a blaze not easily extinguished, a blaze to set her afire, too. . .if she could bear the heat.

Lucy took a deep breath. 'It's nothing so dramatic,' she told him simply, letting her hand lie where it was, in his warm fingers. 'Just a broken engagement, that's all.'

'Ah!' There was a quick intake of breath from the other side of the table. 'But that's not all, is it? That's not enough to make you look so. . .so hunted. Not now so much, it's true, but back in London once or twice I had the impression you were actually frightened. Who is he, this ex-fiancé of yours who's been tormenting you?'

'I don't think his name's all that important,' Lucy said evenly. 'You wouldn't know him, and he hasn't actually been tormenting me,' she went on with a sigh. 'It's just that I'm not sure how he'll have taken my letter. I wrote to him, you see, breaking off our engagement. He was abroad—then. I suppose it wasn't very brave. . .'

She looked up from her perusal of her free hand lying on her lap, suddenly aware of a new tension in the atmosphere between them. Matthew released her hand to reach for the wine-bottle, pouring a full measure into his glass, which he half emptied then set down on the table so sharply that the red liquid spilled over on to the cloth.

He dabbed at it impatiently, frowning. 'So why won't you tell me his name?'

Lucy opened her mouth only to close it quickly again. There was something about the urgency in Matthew's voice that warned her to be on her guard.

'As I said, I don't think it's that important.'

'You're keeping it from me deliberately, so there must be some reason.'

Matthew was glaring at her now, and Lucy was at a loss to understand this sudden flare-up of anger. What had happened to that new, gentler side of him she had glimpsed earlier in the day? Did he think that her story of the broken engagement was nothing but a lie, and that her ex-fiancé was a myth. . .or a rival, still? What could be so important about his name?

'My reason is private, and in case you think the whole thing's just an invention to. . .to give me time,' she said not quite steadily, 'I promise it's all true. Ask Bella if you don't believe me.'

'Of course I believe you.' Matthew screwed his napkin up and tossed it on to his empty plate. 'But don't you see. . .?' His voice dropped, taking on a deeper, more persuasive note which caught at Lucy's heart, making it lurch uncomfortably. 'If we're to become——' he paused a second '——friends,' he said meaningfully, his eyes glittering beneath his dark brows, 'then we shouldn't be keeping secrets from one another.'

'It's not a secret——' Lucy began, desperate now to keep her resolve.

'So. . .why not tell me?'

Lucy took a deep breath and looked at Matthew steadily across the table.

'You know what happens in fairy stories when people insist on being told things they're not meant to know?'

Matthew shook his head impatiently. 'I don't see. . .' he began, but Lucy held her ground.

'Those stories always end in tragedy,' she told him. 'And I don't want to tell you my fiancé's name. Can't you leave it at that? Please, Matthew. I have my reasons, and it's simply not that important.'

'It is to me,' Matthew rasped suddenly, the intensity of his feeling all the more alarming for being kept rigidly under control. 'And if you felt anything for me—as you claimed you did this afternoon—you'd tell me. Still, if that's how you feel, that must be an end to it. I won't ask again.'

He shrugged and pushed his chair back from the table, half turning away from her.

'Coffee?'

Lucy nodded and waited in a miserable silence until the waitress brought the cups from which they drank still without speaking.

If Lucy's emotions had been in a turmoil before they had come out to dinner, it was nothing to the state they were in now. *Why*, she kept asking herself, did it matter so much to Matthew what her fiancé had been called?

She made a last attempt to put the record straight. 'It is all over between us—the man I was going to marry and me,' she told Matthew as they were getting into his car a little while later. 'There's nothing I'm keeping back, Matthew, truly. The relationship is finished. Forever.'

Tears pricked at her eyelids as she spoke the words that sounded the death knell for the very real love she and Stephen had shared. But Matthew either didn't or chose not to see the wetness on her cheek as he drove them home in a brooding silence which told Lucy nothing of what was going on behind those hooded eyes staring intently into the darkness.

But one thing she did know. The intimacy they had begun to share not so many hours ago had clearly been stifled at birth. It had, as Matthew had implied, ended.

CHAPTER SEVEN

THE following morning, after a restless night disturbed by anxious dreams, Lucy woke up weighed down by a feeling of hopelessness she couldn't account for at once. Then she remembered.

What an awful evening it had turned out to be, and it could have ended so differently, too, if Stephen hadn't managed even in his absence to drive a wedge between her and Matthew.

Not a word had passed between them on the journey home. Matthew had insisted on driving, and Lucy half suspected his leg was paining him, too, probably as a result of driving that afternoon, but it was more than her life was worth to say anything.

Instead, she had sat motionless by Matthew's side, staring miserably out at the darkened countryside, still utterly at a loss why this black mood should have descended on him at her refusal to tell him Stephen's name.

Maybe it had been a mistake to have concealed it from him, but Lucy, too, had more than a grain of stubbornness in her, which had made it impossible for her to give in. The more insistent Matthew had become, the greater her determination to remain silent and protect at least this small part of her life from his probing.

Now, lying in bed and listening to the rooks' noisily persistent conversation outside her window, she tried to analyse the reasons for that silence.

At the beginning it had been purely an instinct for self-preservation that had decided her against revealing Stephen's name to Matthew, knowing that the more she told him the greater risk she ran of opening wounds only now beginning to heal. And she had feared, too, that prolonging the discussion would only serve to remind Matthew himself of his own broken relationship, inflaming the bitterness and anger that erupted whenever Celia Trevenn's name was mentioned.

But if that were all, wouldn't it have been better to tell him what he thought he wanted to know, and get everything out into the open? Then their own relationship could be free to take its course—whatever that turned out to be—without being haunted by any spectre of past loves.

Lucy sat up in bed, pulling the bedclothes up to her chin as she hugged her knees, conjuring up the images of first Stephen, open-faced yet inwardly a seething mass of hang-ups and jealousies, and Matthew—dark, brooding Matthew, whose eyes seemed to bore deep into her very soul.

That was it! That was why she had insisted on keeping that one secret from him. Revealing Stephen's name was the one thing he hadn't yet been able to persuade her to do against her will, and this was the only occasion on which she had held out against him.

So many times since their very first meeting, when Matthew had persuaded her to come to live in his house, she had found herself giving in to him, and to keep Stephen's name firmly locked away from him was one weapon in her defence of her own inner self which seemed so vulnerable to his overriding will.

Once he knew everything, she would be unprotected against the power of his personality...and her own desire...

But *that* thought barely had time to surface in Lucy's mind before it was ruthlessly suppressed and banished to the inmost recesses of her untrustworthy heart.

There was no future there—none at all. As though to

demonstrate to her subconscious the strength of her resolve to ignore even the slightest pangs of what might have been, Lucy sprang out of bed and pulled her clothes on. She still had her job to do, after all, though how long Matthew would want her to stay here, now, she still had no idea.

Matthew was already downstairs when Lucy went into the kitchen to make the breakfast, looking as if he, too, had spent a disturbed night.

'The usual breakfast?' Lucy enquired of the broad back standing by the window. 'Coffee and toast?'

Matthew nodded curtly without turning round. 'That'll do. Thanks.'

He remained in his motionless pose while Lucy bustled about in the still unfamiliar kitchen, laying two places at the big pine table and making the coffee and toast—all in a dense silence. In another man, or child, Lucy would have thought this was a manifestation of a fit of the sulks, but in Matthew, so self-sufficient and commanding, it could only be pride making him withdraw so totally into himself—hurt pride at having been thwarted so effectively.

'Breakfast's ready,' Lucy told him brightly, then added with a little smile that went unnoticed, 'and I haven't burnt the toast!'

He swung round then and stared at her blankly, then shrugged as he took his place opposite her, pulling in his chair with a grating noise on the flagged floor.

Lucy sighed as she poured the coffee. Obviously there was to be little communication between them today.

'Have you any plans for today?' she asked in what she hoped was a pleasantly conversational tone. 'Will you want me for anything?'

Matthew flashed her a quick glance from beneath his heavy brows, and something in his expression made Lucy's face grow warm. She could have phrased that question better, under the circumstances, but it would be too obvious to try to amend it.

'No.' Matthew shook his head. 'I won't want you——' he paused significantly '—for anything. You can do as you please. I've got a lot of work to catch up on.'

The total uninterest in his tone struck a chill into Lucy's heart, and she derived little comfort when, a moment later, having drained his coffee, he added only slightly less abrasively, 'I can get my own lunch. You take the car and go off somewhere. You may as well see something of the area while you've got the chance.'

Lucy sighed. 'Have you any idea how long we'll be here?' she asked.

Matthew frowned and tapped the end of his knife against the table. 'Just a day or two. I had intended. . .' His mouth tightened, then his shoulders moved in a gesture of resignation. 'It doesn't matter,' he said shortly, 'but there seems no point in prolonging our stay, does there?'

He lifted his eyes from his study of the table to stare directly at her, and Lucy flinched inwardly at the coolness she saw there.

'No,' she answered in a low voice. 'I don't suppose there does.'

And that was that. Minutes later Matthew left the table and disappeared into the small study near the music-room, shut the door, and then. . .silence.

More depressed by this downturn in their relations than she would have cared to admit, even to herself, Lucy did all the chores, relaid the table for Matthew's solitary lunch, then went to tell him she was about to go, finding him already at his desk poring over a pile of papers.

'You're sure it's OK for me to have the car?' she asked him. 'You won't suddenly find you need it? I could just go for a walk.'

Matthew shook his head. 'I told you, I've got work to do. I shan't be going anywhere.'

He slewed round in his chair. 'Have you planned to go anywhere in particular?'

'Not really. As you know, this is unfamiliar territory to me.' Lucy paused, then added tentatively, 'Is there anywhere you could suggest?'

Matthew frowned and pursed his lips. 'There's Bamburgh, just up the coast, and Dunstanburgh in the other direction. Not much to see, but a spectacular position on the cliffs—and near the sea, of course.' He shot her a swift glance, then went on as though he meant nothing in particular by it, 'But if I were visiting the area for the first time, I'd head straight for Lindisfarne on Holy Island. Only if you do decide to go there, don't get cut off,' he warned her. 'You can only get across at low tide, and I won't be there to rescue you this time if the sea decides to claim you.'

Their eyes met briefly, then Matthew turned away again to study his papers. 'Enjoy yourself,' he said, without looking round. 'And don't hurry back on my account.'

His final words sounded not so much a simple invitation to make the most of her day of freedom as a cold dismissal, implying it was nothing to him whether she was in the house or not, and successfully dampening Lucy's sense of anticipation as she prepared to set off on her excursion.

Her spirits rose, however, as she put the miles between her and Matthew, and, by the time she reached the causeway to Holy Island and discovered that the tide was out, she was feeling much more cheerful.

She wandered over the Priory, soothed by the tranquillity which seemed to pervade the very atmosphere in spite of the evidence of man's bitterness and intolerance all round her in the ruined buildings. She even found she was able to think of Stephen with a kind of resigned regret instead of the foreboding that had haunted her since she had written him the fateful letter.

As soon as she was back in London she would get in touch with him and fix a meeting—if he was willing— and see if they couldn't end their relationship as friends, at least. She couldn't spend the rest of her days being frightened and resentful of him.

As for the other man in her life—Matthew...For the last time, and of her own volition, she would give in to his will and tell him that very evening all about Stephen—by name, if that was what he still wanted— and then make plans for her own future. There was no point in drifting from job to job any longer now that she was free and unattached again.

Maybe she should try a new career altogether, even train for something different...but what?

Lucy sat down on a sun-warmed block of stone and laughed out loud. What did it matter? Anything would do as long as it paid the rent and opened up new horizons in her life.

She closed her eyes, listening to the rustle of the wind in the grass and the cry of the birds wheeling round the ruins, and suddenly she felt, for the first time for weeks, utterly content...

'Better get a move on, love, unless you're planning on staying here a good few hours.'

'What?' Lucy came to with a start and sprang to her feet. 'I must have dropped off,' she told the elderly man who had woken her up and was smiling at her as she collected herself together. 'It's so peaceful here, especially after yesterday's storms.'

The two of them walked companionably back to the car park.

'People often find that,' her new friend told Lucy, 'but then, after all, it's a special kind of place, isn't it?'

Yes, it was, Lucy agreed silently, as she headed back towards the mainland, gratefully aware that even that short visit to the Priory had had a healing effect on her spirit.

Whatever happened she mustn't let her newly regained serenity be disturbed on her return to Rookstones; not by Matthew, not by memories of Stephen—not by anything or anyone.

She stopped at a wayside café for a coffee and a sandwich, hungry suddenly, as she'd missed out on lunch, and drove back in the vague direction of Rookstones, taking any road that caught her fancy, so that it was almost dusk when, with a feeling she couldn't quite analyse—part trepidation, part resignation—she arrived back at the house.

She sat quietly in the car for a while to savour the last moments of solitude, and trying to recapture something of the atmosphere of Lindisfarne to give her strength to face Matthew with equanimity, whatever mood she might find him in. After all, they had hardly parted the best of friends that morning, and he had had a whole day to brood on her stubborn refusal to tell him what he had insisted on finding out.

But she couldn't sit here forever. 'Come on, Lucy,' she said out loud. 'Back to work for you.'

So at last, and with a little sigh of regret, she climbed out of the car and walked briskly into the house.

'I'm sorry if I've been gone for a long time,' Lucy began as she stood in the doorway of the drawing-room, where Matthew was sitting comfortably reading a book by a roaring log fire. 'Goodness—that's an amazing sight! You forget, living in London, what a real fire looks like.'

She crossed over to stand by the fireplace, holding out her hands to the blaze, and Matthew looked up from his book with a smile of genuine pleasure at her return, with no hint, she was relieved to see, of his former moroseness.

'Did you have a good day? Where did you go?'

'I took your advice and went to Holy Island. It's a wonderful place, isn't it? So peaceful.'

She turned and stared at the flames leaping up the chimney.

'Hmm.' There was a soft gleam in Matthew's eyes as he studied the back of her head, but Lucy was unaware of this.

'If I'd known where you were and realised how late it was getting I might have begun to get worried that you'd been cut off.' He uncoiled his long limbs and rose slowly from his chair to cross over to the window to pull the curtains. 'I, on the other hand, have had a very lazy day. I finished my work, or at least as much as I felt like doing, worked for a while in the garden clearing some of the paths. . .'

His lips curved momentarily as he darted a quick glance at the fading scar on Lucy's cheek. 'Then I settled down with this.'

He waved the book which he was still holding, and Lucy saw with surprise that it was the poetry anthology she had noticed in his bedroom that first day she had come to work for him.

'Do you like poetry, Miss Ambleside?' he asked lightly.

'Yes, I suppose so,' Lucy replied absently, not sure quite how to take this change in his attitude towards her since they had parted that morning. 'Some, anyway, but it's not something I sit down and read very often, I have to admit.'

'You should—you really should. There's something here for every occasion—and every mood.'

Matthew came to join her by the fire, leaning one shoulder comfortably against the mantlepiece while he stared meditatively at the book in his hand. 'There's always food for thought, at least.'

Lucy watched him for a while, lost in some reverie she couldn't guess at, and then moved away from the fire, smoothing back her hair from her warm face.

'I won't disturb you, then,' she said quietly. 'There are things I should be getting on with. I'll let you know when the meal's ready. Is there anything special you'd like this evening?'

Matthew smiled abstractedly. 'No—whatever you've got.'

'Steak?'

'Steak will be fine, and we'll have a bottle of wine to go with it. I'll look one out in a minute. Oh, and let's have our meal in the kitchen,' he added when Lucy was almost out of the door. 'I find the dining-room here a bit bleak, with all that heavy furniture.'

The atmosphere in the house had definitely lightened, Lucy thought with relief as she ran upstairs to tidy herself and change out of her jeans into a flowered skirt and soft wool sweater in matching shades of a subtle green which she knew suited her, and, although there wasn't any real need to change, it was a custom she had become used to when she was asked to eat with her employers, as a matter of courtesy.

Matthew was standing by the kitchen table when she came down again, and she could hear the quick intake of breath as he took in her altered appearance, and, although she tried to ignore the appreciative glint in his dark eyes, she couldn't pretend she hadn't noticed it.

He, too, had changed out of the cords and fisherman's pullover he had been wearing all day into dark trousers and a black cashmere polo-neck sweater that accentuated his swarthy complexion, making him look almost foreign, and even dangerous.

She turned her back, snatching up one of Dot's aprons

to tie round her as much to disguise the heightened colour in her cheeks as to attend to the dishes keeping warm in the oven.

'You are an amazing girl,' she heard Matthew remark softly behind her. He poured out a little of the wine and sipped it thoughtfully, then nodded with approval as he filled their two glasses.

'How—amazing?' Lucy enquired with interest, as no further explanation seemed forthcoming.

'You're brought up here, not exactly full of enthusiasm, to say the least, to a strange house. . .no, not brought,' he corrected himself. 'You did the bringing, didn't you, in an unfamiliar car, to an area you didn't know? Then you proceed to settle in with no fuss, organising everything and creating delicious meals as though this were your home.'

He paused, and Lucy felt—no, knew—there was a significance in those last words she'd rather not even contemplate, and concentrated instead on bringing the dishes to the table with a clatter of plates that filled the silence more effectively than any comment of hers.

'And, as if that weren't enough,' he went on, seating himself opposite her, 'you take the trouble to make the surroundings, and your own appearance, as decorative as you can.'

His eyes moved from the posy of flowers flanked by two candles in the centre of the table to her shining hair held in place by a dark green Alice band, then travelled slowly the length of her body and back to rest on her face.

'As I said, amazing,' he repeated softly.

'Thank you, kind sir,' Lucy acknowledged with a bright smile, desperately trying to suppress an acceleration in her pulse-rate, 'but I fear you flatter me. It's my job to be efficient, and I like to make things—well, nice. And if that involves me in coping with unfamiliar surroundings, then I just have to get on with it. This house is no problem, believe me,' she went on, serving the vegetables and handing Matthew his plate. 'You should see some of the places I've been expected to manage in.'

She chattered on as they began to eat, describing some of the more eccentric households in which she had worked.

'So, you see,' she ended, 'compared with all that, working here really hasn't been a problem.'

'Except for the demands of its owner.' Matthew raised his glass and held it up so that the wine shone with a garnet glow against the candle-flame.

'Oh, I wouldn't. . .' Lucy began, but a darting glance from across the table silenced her protest.

'I've been doing a lot of thinking today,' he went on, staring at the glass twirling between his lean fingers, 'and I realised how rude I must have seemed. Your fiancé's name—your *ex*-fiancé's name,' he corrected himself, 'is none of my business. You were quite right and, if I reminded you of things you were trying to forget, I'm very sorry.'

He drained his glass and put it back on the table, not raising his eyes to Lucy's startled gaze.

She sat quite still for a moment to collect her thoughts.

'I've been thinking too, Matthew, and I've come to a decision. I've no idea why my fiancé's name was so important to you. I wouldn't have thought it could have mattered to anyone except me, and I did have my reasons for not wanting to tell you.'

She took a deep breath and fixed Matthew with wide, green eyes that shone luminous in the candlelight.

'His name is Stephen le Breton,' she said quickly before she had time to change her mind. 'And the only reason I didn't want to tell you was that I've been trying to forget him and. . .and everything about our relationship,' she ended faintly.

She didn't know what reaction she had been expecting, but all she heard was a long exhalation of breath as though some great tension was being released.

'So. . .' Matthew murmured to himself, and a veil seemed to cloud his dark eyes as he pushed his chair back and walked slowly over to stare through the uncurtained windows at the black, starless sky, his hands clasped tightly behind him.

'I knew I shouldn't have told you,' Lucy said miserably. 'I sensed somehow it would be a mistake, giving in to you. I knew I should have kept his name a secret, and not just to avoid re-opening old wounds. Why was it so important to you, Matthew?'

Matthew turned slowly to face her, his features a stony mask. 'I had my reasons too,' he said enigmatically as he came back to the table and sat down. 'You haven't told me everything, though, have you?' His eyes narrowed as they rested on her anguished expression. 'I'm not a complete fool, you know, and you might have thought I hadn't noticed the effect le Breton's letter had on you. The letter I found in your flat that evening—it was from him?'

Lucy nodded mutely.

'And it changed your mind about coming back to housekeep for me. In spite of all your reservations.' His eyebrows flicked up in a wry smile, then his face grew serious again. 'You were still scared afterwards, weren't you? It's only since you've been up here that you've begun to lose that hunted look. Come on, Lucy, you can tell me now. . .unless——'

Matthew's eyes flashed at the enormity of the thought that had struck him. 'He hasn't been threatening you, has he? Physically, I mean?'

Lucy shook her head. 'He's never actually touched

me—not in that way. But he's a very jealous man, and I only discovered quite how jealous after we'd got engaged. He accused me. . .well, never mind that. . .' She covered her eyes briefly with her hand before going on in a dull monotone. 'When I decided I couldn't take any more, I wrote to him. Then I got his letter, and I knew he was in London, looking for me. I knew there'd be more scenes, worse ones, and yes, I suppose I did wonder quite *how* angry he might become. But I'm sure he wouldn't. . .'

Her words trailed away at last into an unhappy silence broken by Matthew's low voice.

'I'm sorry, Lucy. I'd no right to ask all those questions. If only I'd realised. . .'

He looked across to where she was sitting hunched up on the wooden kitchen chair, her chin resting on her hand, and his eyes softened.

'Come on, let's go into the drawing-room. It's a shame to waste that fire.'

He got up and came round to Lucy's side of the table, holding out his hand to help her to her feet.

'You go and sit in there, and I'll make some coffee and bring it through.'

His fingers tightened round hers and he stooped quickly to brush her cheek with his lips.

'If Stephen le Breton ever threatens you, ever lays so much as a finger on you, he'll have me to answer to. Remember that, Lucy. I'll be waiting for him—at last.'

Lucy was puzzled by the intensity of feeling in his voice, but she was too confused and upset now to make sense either of her own thoughts or of Matthew's reaction to her story.

'I'll remember,' she said with a wan smile that hardly reached her eyes. 'But I'm sure it won't come to that.'

She walked slowly through to the drawing-room, not bothering to turn on the lights, and knelt down by the fire to replenish the logs, idly watching the sparks fly up the chimney as she poked the embers to encourage a new flame. She felt utterly drained, and yet, at the same time, could sense the beginning of a feeling of release, as though by telling Matthew the whole story of her relationship with Stephen she had been enabled to see it in perspective.

Stephen represented closed chapters in both their lives, and she must try to convince Matthew of the fact.

Almost in a trance, Lucy went on staring into the fire, hypnotised by the constant flickering of the dancing flames, so that she was barely conscious of Matthew's soft footsteps crossing the carpet, and only came to with a start as he placed the coffee-tray on the table by the sofa behind her.

'No point offering you a penny for them,' he remarked lightly. 'It would be stealing.'

There was a bottle of brandy on the tray as well as the coffee, and Lucy watched as he poured out two generous glasses.

'No argument,' he told her firmly. 'This is medicinal. I think we both need it.'

He bent down and placed the glass in her hands, folding her fingers round it, then sat down at one end of the large sofa, facing the fire so that his outstretched legs were almost, but not quite touching her.

Lucy moved so that she was sitting on the floor with her back supported by the other end of the sofa, and gradually a comfortable silence grew to envelop them, broken only by the crackling of the logs in the grate.

'So it really is over, you and Stephen le Breton?' Matthew asked quietly after a while.

'You know it is. I told you,' Lucy said.

'Yes.' Matthew reached out a long arm and touched her cheek. 'But I had to make quite sure before. . .' He hesitated, and Lucy saw a gleam flicker in his eyes like the reflection from a flame, only she knew this fire was not like the one burning in the hearth.

'Before what?' she asked faintly, feeling her heart begin to pound madly in her chest.

'Before I make love to you.'

'Oh. Supposing. . .?'

'Suppose nothing, Lucy Ambleside. Don't go all coy on me, it won't suit you. There's something between us, you know there is. You felt it in the car when I kissed you, and if I hadn't been so pig-headed. . .' He shook his head impatiently. 'Never mind. All that's in the past, and thank heaven there's time now—all the time in the world. Come.'

He held out his hands, the light in his eyes summoning her like a beacon. Lucy was powerless to resist, and she felt her legs move as though of their own volition, slowly yet inexorably, to carry her into his waiting arms.

For a while he held her motionless against his chest, but the racing heartbeats beneath her cheek told Lucy more than the fiercest embrace could have done of the passion waiting to be unleashed, swift and merciless as an arrow from a bow.

Lucy trembled slightly as every nerve in her body tautened in anticipation and the arms holding her tensed in response. Then Matthew's hand moved gently to cup her chin, tilting back her head so that he could look down into her face and search there for the answer he sought to his unspoken question.

'Your eyes are green—green and mysterious as northern seas that could drown a man,' he murmured, stroking back a tendril of hair from her forehead. 'But the shadow's gone—all gone.'

He gave a little laugh and bent to brush her eyelids with his lips, his caress light as a moth, before they moved to her cheek, her neck and then, finally, her mouth, where, warm and hungry, they came at last to take possession of hers.

Lucy's arm wound itself convulsively round Matthew's neck to thrust her fingers through his hair and bring his head closer to hers as she responded with a surge of ecstasy to his kiss.

His mouth crushed hers even more pitilessly, and now his hand began to move from where it had been resting on her back, holding her lightly, to roam over her body, exploring every curve in a sensuous voyage of rediscovery, as though to remind him of all he had begun to learn about her the day before.

Lucy's limbs melted in his arms as she waited, helpless, for any demand he might make of her and, as his hand travelled lingeringly over her to close over her breast, waves of delicious delirium began to break over her and she felt the serpent of desire uncoiling in the deepest recesses of her body, forcing her back to arch to his fierce embrace.

His arms tightenend round her, pulling her across him as he lay sprawled on the sofa, and shamelessly she rejoiced in the hardness of him thrusting against her. Warm hands slid under her sweater to caress the bare skin beneath, making her stomach contract with a violent convulsion that made her cry out with longing.

Matthew's hands lost their gentleness then and pulled the sweater roughly over her head, gripping her shoulders and upper arms tightly enough to leave weals behind on the pale skin—the marks of his desire, Lucy thought with a wave of exultation as, almost shyly, she ran her hand over the hard muscles of his chest and felt them tense to the touch of her fingers.

The straps of her slip slid down over her arms and deft fingers reached for the zip at her waist. Matthew's gaze held hers for a tense, almost breathless moment till, with a gasp of unrestrained passion, he stooped with the swiftness of a bird of prey to press his burning lips to the firm curves of her breasts.

His lips closed over each in turn, tasting and teasing until, at last, he raised his head to look wonderingly at Lucy's naked body cradled in his arms, her pale skin rosy in the firelight.

'I want you,' he said simply, running his thumb lightly over her mouth. 'I want you more than I've ever thought it was possible to want anyone.'

His eyes were glittering now, almost feverish with barely controlled desire, and Lucy felt his body quiver as he waited for her response.

A great tenderness swept over her for this strange, paradoxical man in her arms whom she knew to be capable of such coldness—unkindness, even—and then. . .No one could call him cold now, she thought, with a kind of wild elation at the surging ache his caresses called up from the deepest, most secret parts of her body. And now she, she alone, had the power in her own surrender to captivate him entirely. If she wanted to.

She caught at his hand and laid it on her breast, holding it there as his rapacious fingers closed over it, bruising and merciless.

'I know,' she said with the wise, gentle smile of all beautiful and desired women through the ages, 'and. . . and I want you, Matthew.'

She buried her face against his shoulder and felt rather than heard the slow, racking sigh that escaped him before, with a cry of triumph, the banked-up fires smouldering for so long within him erupted into a blaze that engulfed them both in the searing heat of an unquenchable passion.

CHAPTER EIGHT

LUCY woke to find herself lying on her side, her body curved into Matthew's lean hardness, with his arm, still possessive even in his sleep, lying across her breasts.

She had a dim recollection of being gathered up into a pair of strong arms and carried away from the dying embers of the fire into the darkness of an unfamiliar bedroom, and then. . .

A smile of pure wonder touched Lucy's face as she relived every moment of their lovemaking, the sensual and tender exploration of one another's bodies and the eventual surrender. . .Even the memory aroused a delicious ache deep inside her.

Carefully she stretched her legs down the bed against Matthew's long limbs and covered the hand still holding her with her own, as though to prevent its escape, delighting in the feel of his body alongside hers, his soft breath against her shoulder—the total maleness of him, in fact.

She let her thoughts drift into a state of blissful semi-consciousness, not daring to think beyond this moment. It was enough just to be here, with Matthew, and in his arms.

'Happy?'

Matthew's lips moved against her neck, kissing the soft skin beneath her tumbled hair.

'Very,' she murmured. 'Very, very happy.'

His arms tightened round her and turned her gently to face him. 'That's better,' he grinned. 'I couldn't hear what you said with your back to me.'

Lucy gazed at him with wide-eyed innocence. 'I said I

was very happy,' she said brightly. 'And I hope you are, too, this sunny morning. Did you sleep well?'

'Minx.'

Matthew seized her arms and rolled over to pinion them beneath him, covering her face with an onslaught of kisses that left her gasping.

'That'll teach you to make fun of me,' he observed coolly. 'You ought to have a bit of respect, I hope you realise. It's not every housekeeper who ends up in my bed.'

'I'll try and remember that—sir,' Lucy said solemnly, then exploded into a fit of giggles. 'Not even Mrs Portland?'

'Certainly not,' Matthew said severely, dropping a kiss on to Lucy's nose. 'Mrs Portland is a mature and very dignified lady. Nothing like you at all.'

'No, I suppose not. But I hope I've been a satisfactory replacement, even if I am only temporary?'

'Satisfactory? Oh, Lucy!' The mocking light in his eyes vanished as he pressed his lips to hers in a long, almost yearning embrace that told her more of his feelings for her than even the urgency of his lovemaking.

Lucy slipped her arm round his neck to pillow his head on her breast, and rested her cheek on the springing, black hair—vital and strong as the man she held.

'You don't suppose Dot will decide to come today?' she asked after a while. 'Have you any idea what the time is?'

Matthew groaned and buried his face against her. 'Why do you have to be so practical? You don't have to act the dutiful housekeeper all the time, Miss Ambleside.'

Lucy sighed. 'Habits of a lifetime are hard to break, and I've always been terrified of oversleeping—especially working for you, Mr Fenn. In fact——' She broke off, and Matthew raised his head from its soft pillow just enough to be able to look into her eyes.

'In fact what?'

'In fact I've been terrified most of the time—well, perhaps not terrified, but wary, certainly. You're a very alarming man, Mr Fenn.'

'So I've been told,' he replied smugly. 'It helps keep my employees on their toes.'

'And in your bed?' Lucy asked absently, as though to no one in particular, and was rewarded for her impertinence by such a savage assault by lips and hands that she had to bite back a cry of unfeigned alarm before the storm subsided and Matthew cradled her in his arms as tenderly as though she were a child.

A wave of apprehension swept over her with the new realisation that this man, her lover, was no perfect, gentle knight, but totally unpredictable—a scorpion who might sting even the creature nearest and most dear to him. Pisces, the fish, had no natural defences against such a predator except the ability to swim away through the stormy seas, diving to safer waters until the danger was past.

Even his lovemaking was subject to almost frightening swings of mood, something she would have to learn to accept if. . .

Now her thoughts did begin to edge guardedly towards what the future might hold for her, and where their relationship was heading. Matthew hadn't said anything about any sort of permanent commitment. Was this just a brief affair as far as he was concerned? He certainly had never mentioned the word 'love'. . .but then, neither had she.

And did she love him? What was love, anyway?

Her arms tightened round him and, as though in answer, his lips touched the soft swell of her breast still pillowing his head.

Unseen by those too-piercing eyes, Lucy let her own gaze wander over the man she held so closely, unable for the moment at least to do more than circle round the edges of either of those vital questions.

If love meant wanting him, being hopelessly attracted to him and being happier than she'd been for months, lying here in his bed, then yes, she loved him.

But love went deeper than that. Once she'd really loved Stephen, wanted to spend the rest of her life with him, to make him a home and bear his children. But even that love had been destroyed by Stephen's unreasoning jealousy.

Did she want to commit her life to this other man—dark, secretive Matthew Fenn, whose moods could alternate so abruptly between the aggressive and almost cruel to the tender and infinitely gentle—fire and ice to burn or heal?

Both elements were inextricably interwoven in his Scorpio nature, but for the moment she simply did not feel strong enough to meet the demands that loving him would make on her.

She dropped a kiss on Matthew's dark, rumpled hair, and gently slid her arm from beneath his body, propping herself up on her elbow to look into his face.

With a loving smile that turned Lucy's heart he reached lazily up to pull her head down to his. Their lips met in a long, soft kiss, almost of valediction, and then silently Lucy slipped from his bed and back to her own room.

She'd barely got dressed and down to the kitchen, to begin pottering about in a sort of blissful daze, when there was a knock on the back door and, before Lucy could even get to it, it was flung open by an energetic hand.

'Morning, Lucy. I thought it was about time I put in an appearance again. Not too early, am I?'

Dot's sharp eyes took in the disorganised state of the kitchen—last night's dishes still heaped up on the table and breakfast obviously not begun.

'Slept in, did you? That's nice. You are on holiday, after all.'

'Is it very late?' Lucy enquired sheepishly. 'I never even looked.'

'About ten o'clock,' Dot informed her, twinkling. 'Well, as you haven't finished in here, I'll make a start on the other rooms. I don't want to get in the way.'

She bustled off into the scullery to collect her things, and it was only when Lucy saw her emerge with the vacuum cleaner that she remembered.

The other rooms! Lucy's hand flew to her reddening cheeks.

'Just a minute, Dot! There's something. . .' Lucy ran past her and flew along the passage to the drawing-room, where various items of clothing still lay in disarray on the sofa and floor.

With a quick glance over her shoulder Lucy swept them all up and managed to get up the stairs before Dot appeared in the hall, looking rather mystified.

Lucy hurried down again, and, if her complexion was unnaturally rosy, hoped Dot would put it down to this outburst of energy.

'Just one or two things I left lying about,' she said brightly. 'I thought I'd better put them away before you started cleaning in there. Oh, and we lit the fire yesterday. The hearth probably needs cleaning out.'

Leaving Dot to her chores, Lucy hurried back to the kitchen to find Matthew there pouring out the coffee.

Lucy cleared a space on the table and was just laying out the plates when Matthew grabbed her from behind, entwining his arms round her waist.

'Don't, Matthew! Dot might come in.'

Lucy wriggled to free herself but Matthew held her

tight, nuzzling into the back of her neck beneath her hair.

'What if she does? We've nothing to be ashamed of.'

'No, I know——' Lucy pushed ineffectually at his hands '—but it was private, what happened last night. And there's lots to do. . .' she ended inconsequentially. 'All that washing-up. . .and breakfast. The coffee'll be going cold, and you hate that.'

With a great effort she released herself from her imprisonment and turned to find Matthew grinning at her with a sort of mocking tenderness.

'Always so practical, Miss Pisces. Very well, you win—for now. Breakfast it is, and hot coffee.' With a sigh of resignation he took his place at the table and Lucy brought the toast over.

'Look,' she said proudly. 'Not even scorched—and if ever I had an excuse to burn it. . .'

She caught his eye and they both burst out laughing just as Dot came back into the room.

'Sorry to disturb you,' she said, 'but the rubber band's just gone on the Hoover, and I know there aren't any spares. It's my fault. I meant to get some in, but what with one thing and another. . .'

Matthew stretched lazily in his chair and linked his hands behind his head. 'We'll be going into Alnwick later, and I'm sure one of us can find what you need. Rubber bands, though. . .for a Hoover?' His brow furrowed in perplexity, making Lucy and Dot laugh.

'I know what they are,' Lucy assured her. 'Don't worry, Dot, I'll get them for you.'

'You didn't mention before that we were going to Alnwick,' she commented a little later. 'Any special reason, or just a sightseeing tour?'

'Something I need to get,' Matthew told her uninformatively. 'And it's a nice place to look round. We might have lunch there.'

As they were about to leave Lucy went to find Dot, who was busy brushing down the stairs.

'Is there anything else you want me to get—anything you need, yourself?'

Dot shook her head. 'Don't think so, thanks.'

She straightened up and fixed Lucy with a stare almost as direct as Matthew's.

'I told you, didn't I, pet, that you'd find it here, whatever it was you were looking for? Your eyes. . .' She peered even closer into Lucy's face and nodded with satisfaction. 'The cloud's lifted, hasn't it?'

The shadow, Matthew had called it, the shadow on the sea.

'Matthew. . .' Lucy smiled, then shook her head. 'No, it doesn't matter. I don't know about looking for anything in particular,' she went on after a brief pause, 'but I do know I've felt a lot happier since I came here.' She looked round contentedly. 'It's a shabby old place, but——'

'But it has a peace about it,' Dot agreed. 'And it's friendly, somehow.' She sighed and went back to her dusting. 'It's a pity Mr Fenn's other lady didn't give it a chance. She might have found happiness here, too. . .'

Celia. . . Lucy collected her coat and went to join Matthew, who was already out by the car. He hadn't mentioned Celia again since she had told him about Stephen. Perhaps now, after all that had happened since then, her ghost was exorcised for him once and for all. As Stephen's was for her.

And there was something else that didn't appear to be troubling him so much. . .

'I'm not fussing,' Lucy said casually, though with a mischievous glint in her eye, 'nor nannying you—I wouldn't presume. . .'

Matthew shot her a suspicious look. 'Go on.'

'But it does seem to me that your leg hasn't bothered

you so much since we've been here. I'm actually beginning to wonder whether you really did need me to drive you all this way, or whether it was just a ruse to get me to come.'

'Hmm.' Matthew eyed her consideringly, then grinned. 'I think I'll leave you wondering,' he teased. 'It'll do no harm to keep a few secrets, but you can drive today. Just to keep you guessing, you *and* Dot Weston. Do you think she suspected anything?'

Lucy slid into the driver's seat and backed carefully out into the road. 'I wouldn't be surprised. She's a very wise woman, is Dot. She sees a lot more than you'd imagine.'

Matthew laughed softly and reached out to touch Lucy's cheek. 'It wouldn't take a genius—or a witch— to see the change in you, my love. That light in your eyes and the kissed look to your mouth. . .and that blush.'

Lucy glared at him. 'If you're going to talk like that you'd better take over the wheel. How can I concentrate? I don't even know the road.'

'All right, I'll be on my best behaviour,' Matthew conceded with mock gravity, adding complacently, 'You can't stop me looking at you, though. Why else do you imagine I wanted you to drive?'

Lucy's heart sang with pure joy all the way to Alnwick, and she needed all her will-power to keep her eyes from straying to the man by her side and her mind from reliving every rapturous moment of the night she'd spent in his arms.

Perhaps the mundane activities of lunch and shopping would bring her down to earth. Otherwise she'd have to make sure he drove home, or she wouldn't be answerable for their safety.

'So, what shall we do now?' she asked when at last

they arrived at their destination. 'Lunch first, or shopping? It's quite late, isn't it?'

'Hardly surprising, in the circumstances,' Matthew murmured with an absent-minded look at his watch. He raised his eyebrows in surprise. 'Yes, it *is* late, isn't it? Lunch it is, then. Look, see that pub? I'll meet you there in quarter of an hour. There's just something I want to see to first. Something that won't wait.'

He stooped and kissed her lightly, then walked quickly up the street and disappeared round the corner.

Lucy followed slowly after him, wondering idly whatever was so important that it had to be transacted immediately. Something to do with the house, perhaps, or someone to see who wouldn't be there later?

A hardware shop on the other side of the road reminded her of *her* errand—Dot's Hoover spares. Lucy made her purchases and spent a considerable time browsing round the shelves of what turned out to be a delightful treasure-trove of old-fashioned bits and pieces until a clock striking in the distance reminded her of the time. She must hurry if she weren't to keep Matthew waiting.

She reached the pub with a minute or two to spare by her reckoning and went straight inside, but Matthew hadn't arrived yet so she decided it would be better to wait for him outside, just in case she had come to the wrong place.

She had just reached the door again when someone pushed it open from the other side and strode in past her, almost knocking her aside in his impatience.

Lucy stared crossly after him, noticing at first simply a tall man, brown-haired and in a hurry, then, as he turned to stare at her, she saw who it was—the very last man of all people in the world she wanted or expected to meet.

'Stephen!' she exclaimed faintly, holding on to the

wall for support as she felt her legs threaten to give way. 'Why. . .what are you doing here?'

'Looking for you,' he said with grim terseness as he came up to her, towering over her and blocking the doorway—as a couple of would-be customers politely pointed out to him.

'Move over, squire,' one of them said with a grin. 'Let the dog see the rabbit.' Then, noticing Lucy's sudden pallor, he added kindly, 'You OK, miss? You look as if you've had a bit of a shock.'

Lucy managed a wan smile. 'Yes, I'm fine, thanks. Come on, Stephen, we'd better go outside.'

Giving him no time to argue, Lucy went out into the street again, looking round anxiously for Matthew, half wanting, half dreading his arrival. But there was no sign of him, so, with a fearful sense of foreboding, she turned to face her ex-fiancé.

'You couldn't have meant it!' he burst out. 'That letter—Lucy, tell me it was a mistake. And why have you been avoiding me? I came to see you, to your flat, and you must have got my note. Why didn't you answer it?'

Desperation made his voice rise, and passers-by were beginning to look curiously at the couple clearly having a lovers' tiff on the pavement.

Lucy bit her lip and lowered her own voice almost to a whisper. 'I'm sorry. I know it must have hurt——.'

'You're damn right it hurt! But *why* Lucy? You still haven't told me. Even in your letter, look. . .'

Stephen plunged his hand into an inside pocket and brought out a crumpled sheet of paper that Lucy recognised only too well.

'All you said was that you didn't think it would work, and it was best to end everything now, before it was too late.'

He waved the letter in front of her and took a step

nearer, his face suffused with a mixture of rage and incomprehension.

'Tell me it was a mistake, Lucy. I love you, don't you realise that? And you still love me, I know you do. Come here.'

Taking her completely by surprise, Stephen caught her by the shoulders and pulled her close, then, holding her prisoner, he stooped to crush her mouth with his in what almost amounted to an assault.

Lucy pushed against his chest, but Stephen's strength was too much for her and she went limp in his arms as his kisses became more frantic.

At last Stephen lifted his head, but made no move to release her. 'We'll fix a date, if that's what was worrying you. We'll get married whenever you like. You love me, don't you, Lucy?'

'No, she doesn't.'

'Matthew!' Lucy gasped in relief as Stephen swung round wildly, letting her go at last.

'And what do you know about it—and who are you, anyway? What's any of it got to do with you?'

'The name's Fenn, Matthew Fenn, and I certainly know who you are, Mr le Breton.'

There was an edge of steel in Matthew's voice that Lucy had never heard before, not even when he'd been at his most cutting, and his dark eyes had narrowed to pin-points of glinting ebony. Only a tell-tale pulse, beating furiously high on his forehead just below his hairline, gave Lucy a clue as to the emotions raging beneath his apparently ice-cold exterior.

A slight movement reminded Matthew of her presence in the corner between the pub doorway and the wall, and his eyes softened a fraction as he looked towards her.

'Are you all right, Lucy? This man hasn't hurt you in any way?'

Lucy shook her head, the words of denial sticking in her dry throat, and that seemed to satisfy Matthew for the moment as he turned his attention back to Stephen.

'Lucy doesn't want anything to do with you. I know that for a fact,' he shot at him, 'and if you have any sense, or any pride, left, you'll make yourself scarce and go back where you came from.'

He took a step nearer Stephen, whose face was a study of outrage and fury, but he was not to be intimidated so easily. He turned back to Lucy.

'I don't know what right this man thinks he has to speak to me like that, and it doesn't matter—for the moment,' he added ominously. 'All that can wait. What does matter is that I take you back to London, and I'll get a special licence right away. Then you won't be able to touch her,' he flung at Matthew. 'She'll be mine!'

Both men glared at one another, apparently oblivious of their surroundings or the interested spectators—or of Lucy herself, she began to realise—in what was becoming a battle for supremacy about something much deeper than mere rivalry over her affections, and something she was at a loss to understand.

Still, this was not the place for the full-blooded row which seemed likely to be about to erupt. Someone had to show some sense of dignity.

Lucy took a few steps forward to stand between the two men.

'Don't you think it might be best to go somewhere a bit less public?' she suggested quietly. 'Perhaps we should go back to the house and discuss——'

'House? What house?' Stephen interrupted her, transferring his attention to her once more.

'The house where I'm working as Matthew—Mr Fenn's—temporary housekeeper,' Lucy told him, trying to sound more calm than she felt. 'He had come here on business, and needed someone to share the driving. . .but I can explain all that later. Come on—please, let's go.'

Without waiting to see whether they were following, she set off quickly towards Matthew's car, only to be pulled to a halt by Stephen's hand on her arm.

'My car's behind the pub,' he said, 'and I've no idea where this house of yours is. You'd better come with me and direct me.'

'She's not going anywhere with you,' Matthew began, but Lucy shook her head with a gentle smile at him.

'It's all right, Matthew. And it will give me time to explain to Stephen——'

'Explain what?' Stephen demanded with deep mistrust etched on to his face. 'I thought you were working as this man's housekeeper. At least, that's what you *said*, so what else is there to explain?' he asked with heavy irony.

'And so I am,' Lucy assured him truthfully enough, 'but. . .oh, let's go, Stephen. Please—people are staring at us.'

Lucy felt Matthew's blazing eyes on them as they headed towards the car park, but she didn't dare look round for fear of refuelling Stephen's suspicions, which she must try to allay before the two men met again—not because she cared any longer what Stephen thought about her relationship with Matthew, but because she dreaded the confrontation between the two men. She climbed into Stephen's car, then, before he turned on the engine, moved to face him directly. One misapprehension at least she could put right.

'Listen, Stephen,' she said evenly, as though trying to soothe an angry animal, 'Matthew had nothing to do with my wanting to end our engagement. I hadn't even heard of him when I wrote you that letter. And that's the truth, believe me.'

'Then why?' Stephen exploded again. 'I just don't understand, Lucy. You gave me no warning, just your letter out of the blue.'

Lucy bowed her head and studied her hands intently. 'I know. Maybe that was wrong of me, but I couldn't see any other way of doing it, not then. You were abroad, and if I'd come to see you. . .'

She raised wide eyes to his. 'I was frightened, Stephen.'

'Frightened? Of me?'

Stephen sounded so shocked that Lucy felt a real surge of pity for this man, who honestly did love her in his own way. She tried to hedge, unwilling to confess now, with the drive back to Rookstones ahead of them, how scared his violent outbursts had made her. 'I didn't know how to tell you. . .but what I did was cowardly, I see that now. I *am* sorry, Stephen, believe me, and I had hoped you could come to forgive me, in time.'

'So tell me now,' he rasped. 'Show me how sorry you really are by telling me the truth. You owe me that much, at least.'

Lucy could sense the frustration and anger welling up in him again and laid a pacifying hand on his arm, but Stephen shook it off roughly.

'The truth, Lucy.'

'When we get to the house,' she said in a low voice. 'I'll tell you everything then, I promise.' She hesitated, then added, 'Will you tell me something, first? How did you know where to look for me?'

Stephen shrugged. 'I went to see Bella, when I realised you weren't living at your flat, to ask her where you were.' He gave a bitter laugh. 'You have very loyal friends, I'll say that for them. She refused to tell me where you'd gone, and if I hadn't spotted your letter, lying open on a table, I'd never have found you—not so soon, anyway.'

He turned the engine on and rammed the gear home with a ferocity that made Lucy wince. 'Come on, then. Which way?'

They drove back to Rookstones in almost total silence, but Lucy knew the respite was only a temporary one. If only Stephen could have left things alone, she thought wretchedly. Why did he have to come looking for her, causing them both all this added pain by his refusal to accept her decision? You would have thought that pride alone would have discouraged him from risking a second and even more wounding rejection.

She didn't even dare think of Matthew, and, as for last night, that seemed to belong to a different world, so remote now it might never have existed. . .

Stephen parked in the road outside Rookstones, the car shielded from the house by the thick overgrown hedge, so Lucy had no way of knowing whether Matthew had arrived back or not; but Stephen gave her no chance to find out.

'So?' he demanded roughly. 'We're here now. I want to know everything you were keeping back. Is it him, after all?' He jerked a thumb towards the house. 'If I thought. . .'

His face darkened again and Lucy nodded sadly.

'That's the reason I can't marry you——Oh, not Matthew,' she told him hastily, seeing him leap to the inevitable conclusion, 'but your unreasoning rages. All those times you accused me of having affairs, or wanting to have affairs with the men I was working for—respectable, married men, most of them, with families who liked and trusted me. I knew I could never convince you *you* could trust me, too. Our life would have been one row after another, and I simply couldn't face it. And you frightened me.'

Miserably she studied his shocked expression, knowing there was no way she could lessen the effect of her words. 'I don't suppose you even knew you were being jealous,' she said gently, 'but not being trusted is very hurtful. I couldn't take it any more.'

'But you loved me,' Stephen burst out. 'I know you did. You told me, and I still love you, Lucy. . .so much. . .You must have forgotten. Come here, I'll remind you, make you change your mind.'

Stephen's blue eyes glittered as he grabbed at her arm.

'No, Stephen.' Lucy pushed at him and tried to twist away to clutch at the door-handle, but he was too quick for her and caught her arm to wind it round his neck, holding it tightly to prevent her escape.

Then his other arm went round her, pulling her close as his mouth came violently down on to hers, punishing her for her faithlessness.

'Don't, Stephen!' Lucy cried out, really scared now. 'Please, let me go. You're hurting me!'

'Give me another chance,' Stephen pleaded, gazing wildly into her eyes. 'I never meant to frighten you. I can be gentle too. . .don't you remember?'

His embrace slackened as his hands began stroking her hair, caressing her face, and his lips sought hers now in a soft, persuasive kiss. Lucy's eyes closed in despair, only to open wide with shock a second later as her door was flung open from the outside.

'So this is what you call it being "over" between you?'

'Matthew,' Lucy whispered, horror-struck as she realised how the scene must have appeared to him.

'Yes—Matthew,' he blazed. 'No wonder you wanted me to come back here alone—it gave you just the opportunity you wanted, didn't it? Playing the field, it's called, I believe.'

'It wasn't like that,' Lucy said hopelessly. 'Honestly, Matthew, you must believe me. It is all over——'

'And what's it to you?' Stephen sneered. 'If I choose to kiss my fiancée, that's my business.'

'Your *ex*-fiancée,' Matthew corrected him with icy coldness. 'Or so I've been led to understand. And it is my business, as it happens, since I persuaded Lucy to come up here with the express purpose of asking her to be my wife.'

CHAPTER NINE

DUMBFOUNDED, Lucy stared up at Matthew, but he was already turning away and was walking back to the house when she stumbled out of the car to catch him up.

'Matthew, wait! It wasn't how you imagined it, what you saw—please, let me explain.'

His explanation, about those last words uttered almost casually, would have to wait.

He swung round then with a look of such disgust that Lucy stopped in her tracks to flinch away from him.

'Explain? What is there to explain? And why should I believe any so-called explanation of yours—you little hypocrite?' he blazed, taking a threatening step towards her. 'You swore to me that it was finished between you and — that man——' his gaze swept round to find Stephen, who was following close behind her '—and all the time you were just waiting for the chance to fall into his arms again. I saw you,' he went on, menacing her by his towering presence, 'lying in his arms with your eyes shut as he kissed you. And enjoying every moment of it. I should know how you look then, shouldn't I?'

Lucy flinched at the cruel words, and heard a gasp of outrage from Stephen, but didn't dare turn even to look at him for fear of aggravating Matthew's fury.

Instead, she stood her ground as steadily as she could.

'You're making a big mistake, Matthew,' she said in a low voice pulsing with the desperate effort of making him believe the truth of what she was telling him.

'It *is* all over, I promise you.' She gazed up into his implacable face as she went on, 'It's true that Stephen was kissing me, but if you think I encouraged him. . .'

She paused briefly, then turned to Stephen with an expression of great sadness.

'I'm sorry, Stephen. I did try to tell you, but you wouldn't listen, and now we're hurting one another much more than if you'd never come looking for me. Can't you accept it's over between us—couldn't we just be friends?'

'Friends?' Stephen gave a shout of derision. 'That's what women always say when they're about to betray you with another man. You accused me just now of being jealous, and said you couldn't marry me because I wouldn't trust you. Well, it seems to me I've been right not to, doesn't it?'

He pushed past Lucy to confront Matthew, his clenched fist trembling by his side as though about to connect with the other man's jaw.

'I know she says it was all over between us before she met you, but I don't believe it, and she'd have come back to me in the end. I could have made her happy, but you wouldn't understand about that, a man like you. You can't stand seeing anybody else's happiness without wanting to destroy it, can you?'

Matthew laughed scornfully. 'Equal and fitting recompense for the ruin of a man's career, I'd have thought, Mr le Breton.'

He spat out Stephen's name with a violence that stunned both his listeners, and the astonishment on Stephen's face certainly wasn't feigned, Lucy was sure.

'The ruin of a man's career? Whose career? I've not the least idea what you're talking about.'

Matthew's eyes narrowed as he fixed Stephen with that icy stare Lucy had got to know so well. 'No, you haven't, have you? Well, I'll tell you.'

They had reached the house now, and he leaned back against the wall, folding his arms with a pleasant smile as though he were about to embark on an entertaining story.

'Once upon a time,' he began, 'there was a young man just setting out on his career. Quite a bright young man, as it happened, ambitious and, luckily for him, in this computer age, born with considerable talents in that field.

'He got a job with a new, enterprising company, and was soon making quite a name for himself and the company he worked for, even to the extent that he had received hints of a directorship when he was still only twenty-three, or thereabouts. The world was his oyster, as they say, or seemed to be, until the day when the managing director's son arrived on the scene.'

Matthew paused for a moment to study the ground near his feet with idle curiosity, keeping his two listeners waiting in suspense for the rest of the story, although Lucy, at least, had a horrible suspicion of what he was going to tell them.

She watched him stoop to flick a piece of mud from his shoe before straightening up, still smiling, to continue his tale.

'The young man found before very long that all the projects he'd been working on, and all his best ideas were being discouraged or trampled on or, which was unpardonable, adopted by the managing director's son and passed off as his own.'

The smile began to fade now, and Matthew's hands emerged from his trouser-pockets to clench, white-knuckled, by his sides, as he went on in a steely voice quite unlike the amiable tone he'd used till now, 'You might think our young man should have gone to confront his boss and his son, but he didn't, alas, get the opportunity. For as soon as he began to realise what was happening, he found himself out on the street—literally—after two hours' notice and with no job, and a threat that if he made trouble they'd see he'd never have a job again, not in computing, anyway.'

Matthew straightened up slowly and moved away from the wall to stand intimidatingly close to Stephen as he went on, 'And the possible ruin of a promising career that stood in the way of his own meant so little to the son that he didn't even recognise the young man in question—or remember my name. Did you, Mr Stephen le Breton?' Matthew shot at him with icy venom.

There was an appalled silence.

'You. . .?' Stephen stuttered at last. 'But I didn't know. . .' He ground to a halt and stared helplessly at Lucy, who was looking at him with total disbelief written on her pale face.

'Stephen?' she said slowly. 'Is this true? But why—how could you do such a thing?'

Matthew answered for him with a short laugh. 'Jealousy, Lucy. Jealousy, pure and simple. I'd have thought you of all people would have seen that—*if* all you told me about young master Stephen here was true.'

He broke off to confront the other man again. 'You knew I was more talented than you, and the thought that I, an upstart, might end up more successful in what you considered to be your personal territory was anathema to you. Whether it was you or your father who was ultimately responsible for my dismissal, I don't know—or care, particularly. But a leopard doesn't change his spots in love or business, does he?' he taunted.

Stephen closed his eyes in despair, and Lucy was filled with revulsion and a kind of pity, too, for the man she had once loved, and whose shortcomings had now been unmasked so shockingly and in such humiliating circumstances.

But what could she possibly say to him—to either man, for that matter? She stared hopelessly from one to the other, powerless to help ease their pain, or her own. Then Matthew spoke again.

'So maybe you can understand now how much I've enjoyed seeing you suffer, and without my having to raise a finger. Lucy's done it all for me. I've waited a long, long time to get my revenge—ten years, more or less—and in the end all I had to do was watch you dig your own grave. Honours are even, I think, Mr le Breton.'

A wintry smile spread across his cold, forbidding features, and even in the spring sunshine Lucy found herself shivering at the supremely menacing figure Matthew presented as he stood motionless, awaiting Stephen's response.

'If I say I'm sorry for what happened,' Stephen said in a low but steady voice, 'you would probably take it as an insult. And if I say I had no idea what was going on all those years ago. . .I may have my faults, but cowardice is not one of them. I'm not going to shelter behind my father, whatever the truth of the matter.'

He drew himself up to match Matthew's height and meet the challenge of that black, pitiless stare.

'I feel sorry for you, Matthew, do you know that? To harbour a grudge all this time, even though you've got all the success and wealth you could ever have wanted. . .' He shook his head sorrowfully as a small smile touched his lips. 'I hope it's made you happy, that's all. As for. . .'

His voice shook a little as he turned to Lucy, who was standing transfixed by the welter of emotions surging through her. 'I did love you, Lucy, and I still love you, but if you say there's no chance of us starting again I have to accept it.'

He looked away for a second, and Lucy knew it was to hide the depth of his feelings, but now she felt too numb to do anything but listen in silence as he went on bitterly, 'I don't know what your relationship is with this man—but then it seems I don't know anything any more, doesn't it? Only that the sooner I get away from here the better—for all of us.'

He bent as though intending to kiss her, then realised just in time how unwelcome this gesture might be, and pulled back with a faint, ironic smile.

'Take care,' he said softly. 'You needn't worry that I'll be bothering you again. I'm off to Brazil next week, so you can rest easy and forget me.'

Then, without so much as a glance in Matthew's direction, he swung away and strode out of the gate to start up his car and wrench it round with a squeal of tyres. Lucy stood listening till the sound of its engine grew fainter and faded to nothing in the stillness of the countryside.

There followed a long silence disturbed at last by Matthew's heavy sigh. 'It's a funny thing, Lucy, but all I feel now is a sort of disgust—with myself. And nothing at all for Stephen le Breton, except relief that he's gone.'

He looked quite drained, Lucy thought dispassionately, and the raging fury that had filled her with such trepidation appeared to have been utterly extinguished.

As for her own emotions...She covered her eyes briefly with her hand at the prospect of all the explanations that still lay ahead. She couldn't remember ever feeling so exhausted.

'Let's go in,' she said dully. 'I don't think I can stand here much longer.'

Matthew noticed now the grey, drawn look on her face, and reached out to support her, but Lucy shook her head and moved quickly away. 'Not now, Matthew. There are things we must talk about, and I'm not sure...'

Her words trailed off miserably as she walked past

him into the house to collapse on to the first chair she came to, which happened to be in the kitchen.

For a while she sat there, quite still, frowning down at her hands lying on the table, as she tried to collect her thoughts, oblivious of the tall figure who stood by the window looking down at her bent head with a bleak expression that might, even now, have touched her heart had she noticed it.

As it was, she studiously avoided meeting his eyes as she said in a low, even tone, 'I think I am owed some explanations, Matthew.'

She heard him take a deep breath, but ignored it as she looked directly at him at last with wide, pained eyes almost drained of colour.

'You used me, didn't you?' she said almost inaudibly. 'You admitted you had been waiting—what was it? Ten years? Ten years,' she repeated disbelievingly. 'Ten years watching and waiting for an opportunity to get your own back on one man—and a man who probably did you a good turn, if only you'd realised it, spurring you on to make a success of your own company.'

'Lucy, listen. . .'

'No, Matthew. I need to say this. The desire for revenge can be infectious, and I don't want to spend the rest of *my* life harbouring grudges. You did use me, didn't you? When you saw that letter from Stephen in my flat, and you recognised his writing, you didn't say anything, but you knew if you waited long enough I'd lead you to him, in time, and give you the opportunity you wanted to exact your retribution. I played right into your hands, didn't I—literally?' she added with a bitter laugh. 'You must have been laughing the whole time, last night, knowing that once you'd taken me you had me and Stephen, when he finally showed up, just where you wanted us.'

Ashen-faced, Matthew winced visibly. 'Is that all you think you mean to me? Even after. . .?'

He reached into his pocket and brought out a small package, which he turned over slowly in his fingers before placing it on the table in front of him, making no attempt either to unwrap it or to give it to Lucy—if it was meant for her. Lucy was too miserable to care one way or the other.

'I suppose you think that the reason I gave Stephen for persuading you to come up here with me was another half-truth—just to rub salt in his wounds?'

'What do you mean?' Lucy asked shakily, knowing the answer, but wanting, even in her state of confused unhappiness, to hear him say it again, to her.

'That I was going to ask you if, in time, and when you'd got over the hurt of your broken relationship with Stephen, you might come to care for me enough to marry me,' Matthew said with uncharacteristic diffidence. 'I've known, you see, ever since—oh, almost since that first day when you walked into my life, that there could never be any other woman for me.'

Lucy hunched back on to her chair and stared blankly at the little packet still in its wrapping.

'You still haven't answered my question, have you?' she asked with persistent doggedness. 'Whatever you claim your feelings for me might have been, you couldn't resist using me as bait to catch Stephen, could you?' Her voice rose in desperation as she looked across at him. 'How can I believe that you. . .those other things you told me, about caring. . .all that. . .when you were capable of doing something so deceitful?

'You made me tell you all about Stephen, and how I felt about him, acting the innocent and pretending you'd never heard about him. How could you have done it to me, Matthew? I don't understand.'

Her voice cracked then, and she felt the tears she'd

kept at bay all this time prick her eyelids, and she dashed them away angrily. The last thing she wanted now was Matthew's pity.

But Matthew was lost in a maze of his own and appeared not to notice the visible signs of her distress as he came across and pulled out the chair opposite Lucy's. He sat down heavily, resting his arms on the table to stare out before him with unseeing eyes.

'It wasn't until I saw that damned letter of le Breton's that all the old resentment came flooding back,' he said slowly. 'I'd more or less forgotten what they'd done to me——' He paused, then shook his head. 'No, not forgotten. But even if it wasn't forgotten—or forgiven—it was buried.'

The old fire flared momentarily in his eyes, then died down as he went on, 'But I'd no idea what your relationship with him was, then, and for all I knew that letter could have been anything—just a casual note, even the offer of a job. I didn't stop to work it out. All I knew was that Stephen le Breton was somewhere around and within reach—thanks to your sudden change of mind about working for me. Maybe if I'd stopped to think. . .'

He shrugged. 'Anyway, I didn't, and yes, I suppose I did use you, as you put it. Not very admirable, I admit.'

'And later?' Lucy prompted him remorselessly after he'd fallen into a brooding silence. 'You could have told me then, when you'd had time to think, and when you'd found out the truth about my connection with Stephen.'

Matthew's lips curved in a small, tight smile that did nothing to alleviate the bleakness behind his eyes.

'I couldn't take the risk,' he said simply. 'I wanted you so much, I didn't dare let you know what I'd done. I wanted you to trust me. . .and of course the last thing I expected was that le Breton would come looking for you up here, of all places.'

He sprang up again and began pacing the room,

swinging round suddenly to face her, his dark eyes glittering with a new intensity.

'There's no hope for me now, is there?' He laughed harshly. 'I might just as well have told you everything at the start. I couldn't have made matters worse, could I? He's won again, hasn't he, Stephen le Breton?'

He lunged forwards without warning and pulled Lucy to her feet, pinioning her arms to her sides to hold her tight against him. Lucy felt her eyes being drawn to his as though by an irresistible magnetism, and his breath was hot on her cheek as he searched her face in a wild hope for understanding.

'It wasn't a game or a battle,' she said quietly. 'No one's won, but it seems to me that we've all lost. The best thing I can do is go away now as soon as possible, and maybe in time we can all put what's happened behind us and start again.'

She gazed into his darkening face with infinite sadness. 'Your scorpion's venom has poisoned everything, Matthew—even your own chance of happiness.'

'But I need you——' Matthew began, but Lucy shook her head gently.

'You don't need me any more, Matthew,' she told him, deliberately misunderstanding him. 'Your leg seems quite healed now and you've got Dot here to help. Mrs Portland will be back soon, too.'

'You know that's not what I meant,' Matthew rasped, loosening his grip of her arms to enfold her closely in his, resting his cheek on her hair. 'I need you with me, always. I want you to marry me. That much was true, at least,' he added with a bitter laugh. 'You must believe me. And you can't have forgotten so soon what it was like, the two of us, last night. . . It meant something to you, Lucy, I know it did.'

Lucy's knees buckled beneath her as he crushed her mouth with his, his lips fierce and as demanding as the hands which thrust beneath her sweater to run over her back, lingering on the smooth skin of her shoulders before taking possession of her soft breast, which even now tensed with a surge of desire she couldn't supress against the hardness of his fingers.

'You still want me,' Matthew cried with a laugh of triumph. 'I knew it. I can feel you wanting me. I haven't lost you at all. You're meant to be mine, you belong here, in this house, in my arms. . .'

He bent his head to brush his lips against the warm, naked flesh of her midriff, moving remorselessly upwards. . .upwards. . .until, with a cry of anguish, Lucy pushed against his unyielding chest, twisting away to take him sufficiently off-guard to make her escape.

She stumbled away from him, reaching out to the wall behind her for support.

'You're wrong, Matthew,' she gasped. 'Oh, I know my body wants you. There's no use denying what you felt just then, but I—me—Lucy Ambleside——' she wrapped her arms round her trembling body as if to embrace her inner self '—*I* don't want you. Not now, not ever. I don't belong here, or to you, only to myself.'

Her final words echoed round the walls as, with an incoherent cry of desolation, she turned and fled through the hall, up the stairs and into her bedroom, where she slammed the door shut and flung herself down on her bed.

Silence, broken only by Lucy's dry, panting breath, came edging back to settle round her, comforting as a shawl.

She listened—no, there were no footsteps following her. She was to be left in peace.

She rolled over on to her back and stared up at the ceiling, letting her mind drift, too numbed by the events of the past few hours to try to get her thoughts and emotions into any sort of order and, strangely, it was almost the last thing Matthew had said to her which came to the forefront of the welter of memories tossing around in her head.

'You belong in this house. . .'

A vision swam before her unseeing eyes. She was standing by those steps leading from the french windows, gazing out over a tended and cared-for garden, the house behind her newly decorated and refurnished, restored and lived-in—by her and the indistinct and shadowy man at her side; a tall, dark man whose love she could feel enveloping her even in this waking dream. And there were children, not visible yet, but waiting for her somewhere, just out of reach. . .

With a start Lucy sat up and the idyll faded, leaving her feeling infinitely bereft and alone. A great longing swept over her to recapture just for an instant the joy she'd felt in that dream. . .if it was a dream. It had seemed so real, the scent of the damp garden so vivid, the people almost alive. . .

Almost without realising what she was doing, she swung her legs off the bed and slipped out of the room and down the stairs to the hall, where she stopped, listening, but there was still no sound. She tiptoed to the big room at the end of the passage and sat down at the piano.

From the kitchen at the other end of the house Matthew heard the faint sounds of music drifting through the house and for a moment thought he must be dreaming. Then he remembered. Lucy.

His first instinct was to get up and go nearer to listen to those strange harmonies unlike any he'd ever heard before, but he knew he must leave her undisturbed. That, at least, he could do for her, he thought with a bitter smile twisting his lips.

What had she said? Music—her music—was a means

of release, and now, of all times, she needed that, thanks to him and his overpowering quest for revenge.

He ran his hands wearily over his face and sat back in his chair, straining his ears for the ebb and flow of sound wafting through the old house—like the sea, he thought absently. The sea, deep and mysterious like Lucy herself, and which she had told him she needed as her special element, laughingly but half seriously explaining it was because she had been born under Pisces.

And it had been the sea that had brought them together, him and his water-nymph with the shadowed sea-green eyes, a creature as elusive as the fish which was her sign. And he'd so nearly caught her. . .

The music faded, surged again with a series of passionate, clashing chords like the surf on the beach—and stopped abruptly. Then—nothing. Not even a final cadence or a single note of farewell.

Moments later he heard her soft steps outside the door. There was a pause, then the door opened slowly.

'Matthew, I think I'd like to leave now.'

Matthew raised his head and their eyes met and held on a slender thread of understanding stronger than anything they had shared till now when it was too late, Lucy thought, almost submerged by a tidal wave of misery.

Her resolve almost weakened, but not quite.

'I'll get a taxi to take me to the nearest station,' she told him with a wan smile. 'You don't know where that is, I suppose?'

'Out of the question,' Matthew told her firmly, brushing aside her protest. 'You go and pack and I'll ring BR and find out about trains—if you're sure you want to go?' he ended, hardly daring to hope she would change her mind.

'Quite,' she said quietly. 'It's the only solution, in the circumstances.'

She turned her wide green eyes towards him, and Matthew's mouth tightened briefly.

'Still the shadow,' he murmured to himself, 'and I'd thought. . .' He shook his head. He'd had his chance and now she was lost to him.

He picked up the small package still lying on the table, unopened, and weighed it thoughtfully in his hand before thrusting it back into his pocket.

'Let me know when you're ready to go,' he said distantly, 'and I'll come and fetch your luggage.'

Lucy quickly did her packing, not bothering much with how neatly she did it. Speed was what mattered.

Even so, it was with a sharp pang of regret that she drove away with Matthew from the house she had come to feel a deep affection for, and from the ever-present, noisy rooks still circling their elm-top roosts, completely oblivious of the troubles of the humans far below.

But she said nothing of this to Matthew, who sat beside her in an inscrutable silence. Every now and again she would steal a glance at the strongly marked profile silhouetted against the window, imprinting on her memory the darkly gleaming eyes beneath the uncompromising brows and the firm mouth that had not so long ago been pressed so passionately to hers.

A wave of despair swept over her at the realisation that this would probably be the last time she would ever see him, this intimidating, unpredictable man who could be so tender. It wasn't too late to turn back. She could say she'd forgotten something, and then, once they'd reached Rookstones, find some excuse to stay. . .try to put matters right between them.

She turned to him.

'Matthew?' she ventured timidly, noting his eyes narrow slightly at the sound of her voice.

'Yes?' he said curtly, completely extinguishing the flickering spark of her courage.

'Where are we going?' Lucy asked as she realised the utter foolishness of her earlier notion.

'The nearest station where you can get a train to Newcastle,' he replied in the same brusque tone. 'Then you can get an InterCity to London. You should be able to get the evening train.'

His brows drew together in a frown as he glanced briefly across at her. 'Have you enough money for the journey, and the taxi the other end?'

'Money. . .?' Lucy repeated vaguely. 'I don't know.'

She rummaged in her bag and found her purse, which she shook out on to her knee.

Matthew, watching her out of the corner of his eye, smiled faintly. 'Not much, is the answer, if that's all you've got.'

'I've got my cheque book and a credit card. . . I think.'

Matthew sighed with a kind of resigned exasperation. 'You may be the world's most efficient housekeeper, but you're not exactly the most practical person when it comes to your own affairs. You've never been one for bothering about money, have you? Even. . .'

There was pain behind his eyes as he remembered the difficulty he had had in getting her to name her fee, that day when she had walked so unexpectedly into his life.

'What was it you said once? "Money isn't the most important consideration of my work?"'

Lucy looked across at him with a tightening in her chest. Did he remember everything she had said to him?

She swallowed hard to get control of her voice. 'That sounds horribly self-righteous, doesn't it?' She laughed lightly but not very convincingly. 'But this time I do have an excuse—I was rather rushed into coming away and I didn't think I was going to need much money,' she added not quite steadily.

'You don't have to go, you know,' Matthew said after

a short silence, but there was no hope in his voice, and Lucy shook her bent head again, her dark hair falling across her cheeks and hiding her expression from his sharp eyes.

'I think I do,' she told him quietly. 'I think it's for the best—for everybody.'

Few words passed between them until they reached the station, and after Matthew had helped Lucy out with the luggage he drew out his wallet and a small wad of notes.

'Take this,' he said gruffly, taking her hand and closing her fingers round the money. 'It's not charity. I'm sure I must owe you at least this much salary. Like you, I wasn't exactly prepared to have to settle up so suddenly, but if I owe you any more. . .'

Lucy made a helpless movement with her hands. 'I'm sure you don't——' She looked vaguely at the money he had given her, and smiled wanly at him. 'I'm sure this is too much, but thanks anyway.'

They walked from the car park into the station, where Lucy got her ticket and discovered there would be a train in about fifteen minutes to connect with the London express from Newcastle.

'Don't wait,' she told Matthew. 'Goodbyes are hard enough at the best of times, and I can get a sandwich or something to fill in the time.' She smiled sadly. 'We never did get our lunch, did we?'

A bleak look touched Matthew's face and he took a step towards her. 'I'm sorry,' he said simply, and Lucy knew he wasn't referring to their missed meal. 'I'm sorry for so much, but not for one thing——'

He caught her hands and held them tightly while his eyes travelled slowly down the length of her body and back to gaze into her face, as though drinking every line of her features.

'And I hope you have no regrets either,' he said softly,

careless of the other passengers passing to and fro. 'About one magical night. This is to remind you, just in case you were in danger of forgetting what we shared.'

Before she could make any protest he caught her in his arms and pressed a long, yearning kiss on her mouth, then, without another word or backward look, he turned and strode out of the station, leaving Lucy alone.

CHAPTER TEN

IN A kind of daze Lucy bought herself some sandwiches and a plastic beaker of coffee, then drifted out on to the platform to settle herself on a bench to wait for her train.

She took her time over her snack, concentrating fiercely on every crumb and sip—anything to keep her thoughts from straying to Matthew, though that wasn't easy when her mouth still ached with the imprint of his lips, and everywhere she looked she seemed to see his burning eyes remorselessly following her.

No, it certainly wasn't easy, and, however valiantly she struggeld to keep her misery and her memories at bay, her thoughts would inevitably keep slipping away out of control, and every now and again she found herself looking at her watch, wondering where Matthew was, what he was doing. . .what the two of them had been doing this time yesterday. . .

Angrily Lucy brushed the treacherous tears from her eyes and sat up to stare fixedly out of the train window at the passing scenery; but she didn't see much, only a blur, as she tried to remember how Matthew had deceived her and used her to get his revenge on Stephen. What kind of man, she thought, could do such a thing to someone totally innocent and uninvolved? The sort of man it was best to put as much distance from as possible—as she was doing now, she told herself firmly. She was doing the only thing possible in the awful circumstances that had overtaken her.

Again she found herself staring sightlessly out of the window. This was hopeless. What she needed was something to take her mind off Matthew, Stephen and

Rookstones—a book she could lose herself in, a magazine, anything...but she hadn't any books in her luggage and she hadn't thought to buy one back in the station.

She closed her eyes instead and rested her head against the seat, but sleep wouldn't come, and all she saw behind her closed lids was the firmly etched features she was trying so hard to forget.

'Something troubling you, love? Anything I can do?'

Lucy opened her eyes and looked across at the middle-aged woman sitting opposite her. Lucy had hardly noticed her before, so wrapped up had she been in her own misery, but now she noted the kindly, pleasant face looking at her with such concern that the tears threatened to spill over again.

She smiled rather tremulously. 'No...that is, yes, I suppose it is. But there's nothing you can do, thanks—or anybody. Unless...'

Lucy spied a women's magazine rolled up and stuffed into the bag on the table between them.

'I don't suppose you could lend me your magazine, could you? I came away...' she swallowed hard '...I came away in rather a hurry, and didn't have time to get anything to read.'

'Of course, love.' The woman smiled and pulled out a couple of magazines and a newspaper, all of which she handed to Lucy. 'You keep them, love, as long as you like. Have a good read. Take your mind off your troubles.'

Lucy buried herself in accounts of soap-opera stars' love-lives, mouth-watering and cost-cutting recipes, light-hearted articles on the Royal Family, articles about pets, gardening, travel, and love stories about characters and events far removed, she thought, from the reality she knew, with inevitable happy endings that normally she would have accepted without question, but now knew to be just wishful thinking.

Relationships didn't end with romantic sunsets and wedding-bells. Life just wasn't like that, all tidy and predictable. It was devious and untrustworthy, and so were men—all men, however attractive, however demanding and tender. . .

No! Lucy chided herself fiercely. Keep your eyes on the page and your mind on the words, whatever they are. It's *nice* to have happy endings in stories. Come on, turn over. What's next?

She turned the page and caught the eye of the woman opposite, who smiled at her confidingly.

'It's horoscopes next, dear. As a matter of fact, I always read those first, and she's very good, the woman in there. Things usually turn out as she says, more or less. You read what she says about you—it might cheer you up, you never know. What are you? I'm a Virgo.'

She threw back her head with an infectious laugh. 'Me, with five grandchildren, a Virgo! There, that's better.' She approved of seeing Lucy's answering grin. 'Go on, dear, see what she says about you.'

Left to herself, Lucy would hastily have skipped the horoscopes, but with her new friend's anticipation to be satisfied she felt it would be churlish to disappoint her, so with a little sigh she ran her eye quickly down the page.

'Pisces, watch out for tempests threatening to ruffle the calm waters you fish need for your survival. Hide, if you can, till the storm's over and you can reach a safe haven.'

Lucy stared at the words, which seemed to be dancing a little jig of their own—a jig of triumph, maybe, at their accuracy. Coincidence, she told herself crossly, that's all it was. There was no truth in these things, which were concocted over the breakfast-table by a businessman with a train to catch, as likely as not.

As though to prove her point Lucy gritted her teeth and found Scorpio, and read on in mounting disbelief.

> 'Revenge can be sweet, but guard against using your lethal sting against those you most care about.'

'Lethal sting. . .' she read again, and her mind went back to the last time she'd met Nick, Bella's brother with the fascination for the stars. What had he said? She couldn't remember exactly, but it had been something warning her against the scorpion's fatal sting. And he had held something back, too, she was sure, something he had known about the Scorpio character that he knew might alarm her even more.

Revenge. That was it—the motivating force behind all Matthew did and thought and, no doubt, behind the ambition and single-mindedness that had driven him on to make a success of his own company to rival and overtake that of the le Bretons.

But that wasn't enough. He needed to exact a more personal retribution for the humiliation he had suffered at their hands. And she, Lucy, had unwittingly provided him with just the opportunity he had been waiting for all these years, never in a hurry, biding his time, but confident that in due course he'd get his chance to strike home.

There were other things she remembered, too—his veiled threats against the skier who had caused his accident, his barely restrained anger towards Celia. They, too, might come in for the same ruthless treatment if they were foolish or unlucky enough to run across him again.

And what about her? Wouldn't Matthew consider she was betraying him, too, by what he would see as her desertion? Might not his desire for revenge be stronger than those other, more tender feelings he claimed he had for her, and impel him to come seeking her out to exact it in ways she could scarcely imagine?

Already she had felt the scorpion's sting, and it had killed her happiness stone dead.

Lucy leaned her head back against the seat and closed her eyes as a new wave of misery swept over her. Was it only *last night*, she wondered in amazement, that she had known such rapture in Matthew's arms? So much had happened since then to cloud her memory. . .

How could Matthew have used her so callously if he had really cared for her? Sure, he was attracted to her, but that was all, she could see that now. It had been nothing more than an overpowering physical urge that had driven him to make love to her, and as for those things he had said about needing her and wanting her to be his wife. . .How could she have been so gullible?

She sat up and pushed the papers across the table with a brittle smile.

'Thanks for lending me these,' she said brightly, 'and you were right. Those horoscopes did seem to be uncomfortably accurate, but I don't think they can help much, not as things are.'

'So what sign are you?' the woman persisted, opening the magazine and riffling through the pages.

'Pisces,' Lucy replied with a sigh, wishing she'd leave the matter alone, but not liking to tell her when she'd been so kind.

'Pisces.' The woman pursed her lips and nodded sagely as she read Lucy's horoscope. 'Storms don't last forever, love. They blow themselves out in time, and often things are fresher and brighter after. Silver linings, remember?'

'I know.' Lucy leaned back in her seat. 'But this particular tempest was more of a hurricane. The sort that destroys everything in its path. Still, it's kind of you to care.'

'Well, I hope you find your safe haven,' her friend told her, reaching over to pat Lucy's hand. 'It's not right for anyone so young and pretty to look so careworn.'

Careworn, Lucy thought later as she let herself into her flat. That described her feelings exactly. Tomorrow she'd begin making plans for the rest of her life, but for the moment she felt too exhausted even to unpack. That, too, could wait for the morning.

She slept better than she had had any right to expect and, although she hardly felt refreshed when she woke up, she felt able, more or less, to face the day and the decisions she'd have to make; but there was no hurry, not today. For once she had only herself to think of, and she could take her time.

So it wasn't until late morning that Lucy began to unpack — a job she disliked at the best of times, and now, with all the memories flooding back at the sight of the clothes she'd worn that evening by the log fire...on the beach, at Lindisfarne...

A lump came into her throat which she desperately tried to ignore, and she flung her clothes out of the case on to the bed and began stuffing them anyhow into the bottom of her wardrobe until she had better control of her emotions.

It wasn't until she had got right to the bottom of the case that she found it, tucked among her shoes—the little package she had last seen on the table at Rookstones. The package Matthew had bought yesterday. Yesterday? Lucy looked bemusedly at her watch. Could it only have been twenty-four hours ago that she had been driving to Alnwick with Matthew beside her and her heart singing with joy? Only twenty-three hours since Stephen's arrival had shattered her happiness forever?

Lucy sat on her bed turning the little parcel over in her fingers as Matthew had done, picturing him slipping it into her things when he'd gone to fetch her luggage, and wondering what to do with it now she'd found it.

Her first instinct was to send it straight back to him unopened, but, as she sat there staring at the design on the wrapping-paper, curiosity finally got the better of her.

It wouldn't do any harm to see what was inside, would it? Then she could send it back with a suitable note of rejection.

Very slowly she undid the parcel, her fingers now almost reluctant to reveal what it was Matthew had bought for her. Her words went back to those words he'd flung at Stephen. 'I've brought her here to ask her to be my wife.'

It couldn't be a *ring*, surely? The box wasn't the right shape, for a start.

At last she held it in her hand, the unwrapped box with a jeweller's name on the lid, and gingerly she opened it.

As soon as she saw it, Lucy knew at once why Matthew had bought it for her, this slim oval pendant of an opaque greenish stone set in a silver mount. At least, it looked opaque until she held it up to the light. Then it became translucent, the colour of the North Sea when the sun, unclouded, struck glints from the ever-shifting waves, the colour of her own eyes gleaming in the light of a log fire as she looked into the face of the man she loved. . .

'Oh, Matthew,' Lucy cried brokenly, and the tears she had held back so valiantly the day before now burst through her defences to pour, unchecked, down her cheeks.

'Matthew,' she whispered again, clutching the pendant tightly in her fingers. 'I love you.'

And he really had cared for her. This luminous green stone told her that more than the most priceless diamond could have done. She slipped the silver chain over her head and felt it slide down her neck to settle between her breasts, cool and comforting, too, in a strange way, as though all were not quite lost.

Yet how could it be anything else? Lucy sat motionless, her hand covering the pendant, trying to make some sense of the welter of confused emotions now threatening to overwhelm her utterly.

'I love him,' she said brokenly, 'and I never knew it.'

But that wasn't true, not if she were strictly honest with herself. Of course she'd known it, she just hadn't wanted to admit it—not deep down—nor lay herself open to the storms and anguish that loving a man as complicated and as dominating as Matthew would bring to threaten the peace of mind she had always so jealously guarded.

But what use were mere peace of mind and a tranquil heart undisturbed by love?

Lucy drew out the pendant again, warm from its resting-place against her skin, and held it to her lips.

No use at all, she knew that now, when it was too late. It *was* all over, whatever the stone in her hand tried to tell her. That one night in Matthew's arms was the beginning and the end of what might have been, and now she had to face the rest of her life with only this green stone to remind her of the tempestuous, challenging, passionate man who had been her lover so briefly.

For he would never come looking for her either to seek revenge or to try to put the clock back. She knew that without a shadow of a doubt. He had been hurt once, by Celia, and he was too proud a man to risk humiliation a second time.

Lucy kissed his gift once more and slipped it back inside her shirt, then, with a sigh so deep it seemed to come from her very soul, she got to her feet and went to stare out of the window.

There was another world out there, she noticed almost with surprise. There were people walking up and down totally unconcerned by what she was going through—elderly ladies chatting, children kicking a ball, a dog trotting purposefully along minding its own business—and it was time she went out to join them. Nothing would be gained by sitting in here alone. Brooding wouldn't bring Matthew back. What she needed was work to take her mind off the emotional turmoil that might so easily overwhelm her if she allowed herself to remain unoccupied much longer.

Although Lucy usually found jobs through personal contact and recommendation, there was an agency she used occasionally. She'd visit them now, before she changed her mind, and take the first assignment they could offer her, wherever and whatever it was.

She forced herself to cross over to the mirror to check on what ravages her heartache had wrought on her appearance, and she blenched at the sight of the red eyes that stared back at her, the tear-stained cheeks and disordered hair.

That face would hardly impress anyone, she thought despairingly, almost hypnotised by the miserable stranger she was looking at. Where was the cool, efficient organiser of other people's households? This wretched, waif-life creature didn't look capable of organising anything, even her own life. There was a lot to be done to repair the damage, and it was about time she began.

A couple of hours later, elegantly dressed and made-up, Lucy presented herself at the agency, to emerge minutes later clutching an address of a villa in Greece and a cheque to cover her air fare to Athens on the soonest possible flight.

'Oh, Miss Ambleside,' the woman in the agency had

said with heart-felt relief in her voice, 'it must have been providence that sent you in here today.'

Only if providence is called Matthew, Lucy thought with a pang, but she merely smiled and listened while the woman told her of the clients who desperately wanted someone to come out to the villa they were renting in Greece.

'The wife's recovering from an emergency operation, I gather,' this woman had told her. 'She doesn't need nursing, but she needs someone to organise the family. The husband's an artist, out there to finish a special commission. . .I don't think there should be any problems, but he can't spare the time to cope on his own. Oh, and it's for a month. Can you manage that?'

'It sounds ideal,' Lucy said decisively. 'I was hoping to get away from London——' and England, and Matthew. . .and everything, she thought with relief as she hurried on to the bank and travel agent to get things arranged as quickly as possible, and feeling the fates were on her side for once as she managed to get a cancellation on a flight the following day.

From then until the moment she took her seat in the plane Lucy hardly had a second to think about anything other than her preparations for this trip which had landed so fortuitously in her lap.

She decided not to tell anybody this time where she was going—not even Bella, who probably thought she was still in Northumberland—but, just in case anyone should need her, in some sort of emergency, she left the name and address of the agency on her kitchen table. Then, locking the door behind her, she set off, with a sense of release, for a month of total anonymity.

Lucy had only been to Greece once before, with her schoolteacher parents and in the height of summer, and had remembered it as being fascinating, crowded and extremely hot, so she was quite enchanted by the mass of flowers and comparative emptiness of the countryside around the villa on the coast near Návplion.

Her employers, the convalescent Joanna Vane and Chris, her painter husband, were charming and very undemanding, as were their two children, who were old enough to be largely independent and not yet too much of a worry, Chris laughed when he introduced them; and Lucy soon began to feel like one of the family—a sort of competent older sister, who wasn't expected to do more than cope with the catering and general running of the house. All the washing and housework was done by Maria, a girl from the nearest village, who also advised Lucy in eccentric broken English what to buy and where the best places were to shop.

Apart from that, Lucy didn't appear to have any specific duties, so one day, when she'd finished her chores and the children seemed at a loose end, having already been to the beach once that day and long since exhausted the possibilities of the locality, she suggested driving them in the Vanes' hire car to some of the ancient sites near by.

'Dad was going to take us,' Sophie, the elder, told Lucy as they set off for Mycenae early one morning to beat the crowds, 'but he's always busy, and with Mum having to rest. . .' She pulled an awful face and her brother, Thomas, went on,

'It would have been so boring if you hadn't come, Lucy. We'd have been mooching about in the villa all the time on our own, and the beach is nice for a bit, but that gets boring, too, after a while.'

'You thought going to all these old sites was going to be boring, didn't you? It was only when Dad threatened to send you back home that you decided to come with Lucy and me,' Sophie reminded him. 'We're missing a whole week of school, you see,' she confided to Lucy.

"Cos of Dad's work. Miss Eddery thought it would be OK because Greece is educational.'

'I see.' Lucy smiled down at Sophie. 'And so it is, very, but I hope you're having fun too. I know I am.'

Sophie was quiet for a moment, then commented, her face quite serious now, 'It's funny work, what you do, isn't it? Looking after other people's families. Do you enjoy it?'

Lucy grinned. 'Most of the time, and especially when I've got a family like yours to look after, and in a place like this.'

She drew up by the side of the road where there was an old man selling oranges by the netful, and sent Thomas, under protest, to buy some.

'I won't know what to say,' he wailed. 'Why me, why not Sophie?'

'Because it's educational,' Lucy told him gravely. 'Here, take this money and say, "*Portokalia, parakalo.*" He'll know what you mean.'

Lucy and Sophie watched as Thomas set out bravely on his mission, a solid little boy, tanned and mop-haired and attractive enough to make Lucy's heart lurch with a sudden longing for children of her own.

With uncanny intuition Sophie asked suddenly, 'Why haven't you got a family, Lucy? I heard Daddy talking last night to Mum, and he said he couldn't understand it, you so pretty and good at looking after us. Mum said perhaps you were nursing a broken heart——Oh, look, there's Thomas coming back, and he's got the oranges!'

Lucy hoped Thomas's arrival with his purchases would change the subject, but she was wrong.

'Have you, Lucy?'

'Has she what?' Thomas asked interestedly as he climbed back into the car. 'Have you what, Lucy?'

Lucy smiled resignedly. 'Sophie was asking if I had a

broken heart,' she said, putting the car into gear and setting off for Agamemnon's citadel.

'Pooh, that's silly! Hearts can't break. They're made of muscle,' Thomas scoffed. 'We had one at school—ugh, the smell!' He pulled a terrible face and made suitable noises to match, and Lucy saw her chance.

'I think that's enough of this conversation, Thomas, and for your information my heart's all in one piece, thank you, Sophie, and not even bruised.'

Which wasn't quite true, Lucy thought later that day as she sat alone on the beach going over the events of the day, relaxing while the children amused themselves back in the villa.

She often came down here in the early evening to enjoy a few minutes on her own—but only a few or she would find her thoughts inevitably drifting back across the hundreds of miles that separated them to wonder what Matthew was doing now...whether he was still at Rookstones or back in London...whether he was thinking of her, whether *his* heart was bruised...

It had been a beautiful day, sunny and pleasantly hot, and the sea, still at this time of the year too cold for a swim, stretched away to the horizon in a sheet of brilliant colour—jade, turquoise, ultramarine—ever-shifting and utterly magical, and as unlike the subtle shading of the North Sea as could be imagined by the most gifted artist.

Almost unthinkingly, Lucy reached inside her sun-top for the pendant, which she only took off to go to bed, to slip beneath her pillow, and held it up to the sky to let the light filter through the sliver of stone so that it gleamed with a soft green luminosity of its own.

She held it briefly to her lips before her fingers closed round it, then she drew up her knees and hugged them as she started out over the Aegean, which for once seemed to have lost its ability to ease the ache which hovered constantly round her heart.

Lucy's lips curved momentarily as she remembered Sophie's concern, but the smile didn't reach her eyes, which filled suddenly with the tears that so often threatened when she was alone and off-guard.

Matthew. . .Chastising herself impotently for her weakness, Lucy let the image of his face slide between her blinded eyes and the sea, letting her thoughts dwell on the strong, uncompromising features she'd come to know so well. . .his mouth which could be so forbidding and so gentle, the black brows shadowing those eyes that had seemed able to plumb the very depths of her own being—dark eyes that had had the power to hold her captive even against her will, until that last day when she'd broken free. . .if freedom meant merely a physical separation from the man who had hurt her so much by his ruthless search for revenge.

But he had been hurt, too, and, if she'd given love a chance, might it not have proved to be the antidote to the scorpion's deadly venom? But there was to be no second chance. As for freedom. . .

Lucy laughed silently, a bitter, sardonic laugh. What sort of freedom was it that kept her in thrall to the memory of a pair of strong arms entwined around her, lips and eyes that had swept her away with a passion so intense that it woke her in the nights with its unsatisfied yearning?

And all she had left was her memory and this stone, as cold and lifeless as her heart.

The colours of the sea were softening now to gentler tones, but the water was crystal-clear in the sun's setting light, and still Lucy sat on, staring out to the horizon at the waves' edge, lost in a world of her own.

There were still a few people about, so she didn't take any notice of the footsteps behind her which approached, then stopped a little way off to hesitate briefly before moving on again, a little nearer.

It was only the long shadow cast on the translucent green of the sea that made Lucy aware at last that there was someone standing behind her, someone very tall and still, and for what seemed an age she sat transfixed, gazing at the gentle movements of the waves, not daring to turn. Then the figure crouched slowly beside her, moving aside the dark curtain of her hair with one caressing finger.

Lucy's heart leapt into her throat as she spun round, hand to her mouth and eyes wide with shock. Then she swayed and the sea and sky seemed to swirl about her in a wild dance.

'Matthew?' she breathed, thinking she was hallucinating, then, as a pair of strong arms caught and held her, she knew he wasn't just a vision summoned up by her longing and, at the same time, any last vestige of doubt that it might have been the overriding Scorpio desire for revenge that had brought him here was banished forever by the light of infinite tenderness in the dark eyes she thought she would never see again.

'Matthew,' she repeated slowly, too dazed to say any more.

Matthew didn't speak for a while but stayed kneeling by her side, clasping her tightly with his lips pressed to her hair.

Lucy could feel his heart pounding against her body, the rapid tattoo matching her own racing pulse, and she clung to him in an agony of desperation, praying he had really come to find her, that he wasn't going to disappear before she had time to tell him. . .

'Matthew,' she said again, as though his very name were a talisman to keep him by her side. The word came out as an incoherent sound muffled by his chest, and she moved within the circle of his embrace, which eased just enough for her to lean back and gaze up into his face, noting its lines tauten with a hidden and suppressed emotion she could only guess at.

'There's something I need to tell you,' she said quietly in a voice urgent with feeling. 'Something I think I've known a long time, only I was too blind to see it. And since I've been here. . .' She paused and closed her eyes for a moment before going on. 'I never thought I'd see you again or be able to say it. . .'

She could feel a long, shuddering sigh shake the hard body still pressed against her own, and tentatively, almost shyly, she lifted her hand to rest it against Matthew's cheek.

Before she could go on he put a finger gently against her lips to prevent her from uttering the words burning in her throat.

He hadn't said anything until now, and when he spoke his voice was hoarse and low. 'Don't, Lucy. There's something I need to say first.'

He got up and held out his hands to draw Lucy to her feet, the only outward sign of the passion smouldering inside him the fevered clasp of his fingers round hers and the brilliance of his dark eyes.

'When I saw that train take you away I felt that life had lost its meaning.'

'But I thought. . .' Lucy began, but Matthew, knowing what she was about to say, shook his head.

'I sat in the car until I knew you'd gone. Just in case——'

'In case I changed my mind and came back. But I thought you had driven straight back to Rookstones.'

'Well. . .' The word came out as a sigh, followed by a long silence. 'I knew then that you'd never come back,' he went on at last, 'and why should you, after all I'd done to you? Why should you ever forgive me, let alone care for me?'

Lucy held her breath, hardly daring even to move as he went doggedly on.

'The only grain of hope I could find was in the fact that you hadn't returned my pendant.'

His eyes dropped to the neck of her sun-top and the chain disappearing beneath it, and very gently, as though hardly daring to claim the right to touch her, he drew the stone out from its resting-place between her breasts and held it to his lips.

'For all I knew it might still be lying unopened in your case, or at the bottom of your dustbin. . .Anyway, there was only one way to find out, and first I had to find you. I persuaded Bella to let me have your key. . .'

For the first time his face lightened with a small grin. 'I was desperate by then, and I think she thought she had a madman on her hands, but she's a good listener, I'll give her that. I found myself telling her everything—or maybe not quite everything,' he added softly, letting the pendant fall from his fingers, and running his hand up Lucy's back to the nape of her neck beneath the fall of dark hair, making her heart race painfully by the sensuousness of his caress.

'She agreed, in the end, to let me into your flat, where I found the agency's address. That was yesterday. . .and now. . .'

His hand slid over her shoulder to rest on the curve of her breast, covering the pendant again, his eyes urgently questioning.

'But you are wearing it, and that gives me hope—not that I deserve it—that maybe you think about me a little, even that in time you could come to forgive me?'

Lucy smiled tremulously up at him. 'I've worn it ever since I found it,' she told him shyly. 'I think it's the most beautiful thing I've ever seen.'

'Not a millionth part as beautiful as the girl wearing it. The girl whose green eyes have disturbed my dreams and all my waking thoughts. The girl I want as the keeper of my house for all time—as my wife.'

'Oh.' Lucy's little, broken cry and radiant smile told Matthew all he needed to know as she lifted her face for his kiss.

A long while later Lucy asked, her eyes wide and innocent, 'What did you come all this way for? Just to see if I was wearing your pendant?'

Matthew looked surprised. 'Haven't I told you?'

'Not in so many words.'

'"So many words" would be too many,' he replied softly. 'Three will do for now. I love you.'

Another long silence followed till Matthew moved back a small step.

'Look at me,' he commanded her, reaching out to tilt her head back. 'I need to know something.'

He gazed long and hard into Lucy's eyes, which were shining now, not with tears, but with a rapture she had never thought possible, and he nodded slowly.

'No doubts, not any longer,' he murmured with a smile of great tenderness. 'And I'll see no shadows fall between us ever again, my dear, dear love.'

Lucy touched his cheek. 'There was something I wanted to tell you, and you never let me finish. Can I tell you now? It's very important—for me.'

Matthew made as though to fold her in his arms again, but she grasped at his hands to stand facing him. 'I need to say it, although you know what it is, because I want you to hear the words.'

Her whole face seemed to light up as she looked at him—her fierce, vengeful yet infinitely beloved Scorpio, whose fatal sting she alone, Pisces the elusively feminine, had the power to disarm.

'I love you, Matthew. I love you with all my heart and soul and body, and I can think of no greater happiness in the whole world than to be your wife.'

Almost overwhelmed by the intensity of her own emotions, she turned away, holding tightly on to his hand, to stare out at the sea, her strength and comfort, still shimmering in the evening light.

'Look,' Lucy said, turning to Matthew. 'Our two shadows, side by side.'

As they looked, a small fish swam into the shallows, fracturing the dark shapes into a myriad sparkling fragments until it moved off again into deeper waters and the two shadows merged at last into one.

STARGAZING

YOUR STAR SIGN: **PISCES (February 20th–March 20th)**

PISCES is ruled by the planets Jupiter and Neptune, and is the third of the Water signs, which makes you restless, indecisive, intense and sensitive. You are highly imaginative and idealistic, with a tendency to daydream and to 'switch off' when a difficult situation arises.

Pisceans are kind, charming, sympathetic and true Good Samaritans—but you can sometimes let the needs of others overwhelm you. With your strong need for quiet and privacy, you are very much the home-lover, although your family may exploit your kindness and gullibility by leaving you with all those really nasty tasks around the house!

Your characteristics in love: The most romantic of all the star signs, Pisceans have high expectations of love. You really enjoy the courtship stage of a new relationship but you tend to idealise your lover and to fall in love with a vision, not real flesh and blood. Unfortunately, although you'll try to turn a blind eye to your lover's inadequacies and transgressions, your illusions are often shattered when reality rears its ugly head.

When you do find your ideal mate, however, you are a caring, intuitive lover, revelling in both the physical and spiritual aspects of the relationship. If you are ever unfaithful it is only in your vivid day-dreams and fantasies!

Signs which are compatible with you: You can find harmony with **Cancer**, **Scorpio**, **Capricorn** and **Taurus**—but enjoy a challenge with **Gemini**, **Virgo** and **Pisces**! Partners born under other signs can be compatible, depending on which planets reside in their Houses of Personality and Romance.

What is your star-career? Pisceans aren't always a walk-over: you can surprise colleagues by being very dominant at work, demanding attention and delegating with confidence. Although not very practical, your interpretive skills and intuitive ability to make money in creative fields make Pisces excel in photography, music, theatre and dance. Alternatively, your unselfish devotion to others and to your work may encourage you to gravitate towards a career in nursing, counselling, religion or education.

Your colours and birthstones: Dreamy Pisceans love the pretty, soothing shades of pale blues, greens and violets.

Your birthstone, the amethyst, is also said to have a calming effect, which makes it ideal for restoring harmony to your sensitive temperament. This purple-red stone is also said to ward off contagious diseases and to prevent the evils of drunkenness!

PISCES ASTRO-FACTFILE

Day of the week: Thursday.
Countries: Tonga, Tanzania, Portugal.
Flowers: Water lily, white poppy.
Food: Melon, white fish, mushrooms; your idealism makes you chose pure, natural ingredients where possible. Pisceans don't slavishly follow recipes, but allow their creative skills full rein when cooking.
Health: You are prone to bunions, chilblains and other foot problems—and do keep an eye on your alcohol intake and your weight! Highly strung Pisceans might find that massages, or philosophical regimes such as yoga or t'ai chi, will help them relax.

You share your star sign with these famous names:

Elizabeth Taylor	Michael Caine
Liza Minelli	Bruce Willis
Jilly Cooper	Earl of Snowdon
Julie Walters	Paddy Ashdown
Dame Kiri Te Kanawa	Rudolf Nureyev

Mills & Boon

STARSIGN ROMANCE

DON'T MISS

HUNTER'S HAREM

By

Eleanor Rees

Next month's
exciting new Starsign Romance
featuring Aries.

It has a brand new cover
and celebrates the start of the second year for
this successful collection of scintillating
romances.

Published: March 1992   Price: £1.60

Available from Boots, Martins, John Menzies, W.H. Smith,
most supermarkets and other paperback stockists.
Also available from Mills & Boon Reader Service, PO Box 236,
Thornton Road, Croydon, Surrey CR9 3RU.

ESPECIALLY FOR YOU ON MOTHER'S DAY

OUT OF THE STORM - Catherine George
BATTLE FOR LOVE - Stephanie Howard
GOODBYE DELANEY - Kay Gregory
DEEP WATER - Marjorie Lewty

Four unique love stories beautifully packaged, a wonderful gift for Mother's Day - or why not treat yourself!

Published: February 1992   Price: £6.40

*Available from Boots, Martins, John Menzies, W.H. Smith, most supermarkets and other paperback stockists.
Also available from Mills & Boon Reader Service, PO Box 236, Thornton Road, Croydon, Surrey CR9 3RU.*

Accept 4 Free Romances and 2 Free gifts

•**FROM READER SERVICE**•

An irresistible invitation from Mills & Boon Reader Service. Please accept our offer of 4 free Romances, a CUDDLY TEDDY and a special MYSTERY GIFT... Then, if you choose, go on to enjoy 6 captivating Romances every month for just £1.60 each, postage and packing free. Plus our FREE newsletter with author news, competitions and much more.

**Send the coupon below to:
Reader Service, FREEPOST, PO Box 236, Croydon, Surrey CR9 9EL.**

--- NO STAMP REQUIRED ---

Yes! Please rush me my 4 Free Romances and 2 Free Gifts! Please also reserve me a Reader Service Subscription. If I decide to subscribe, I can look forward to receiving 6 new Romances every month for just £9.60, postage and packing is free. If I choose not to subscribe I shall write to you within 10 days - I can keep the books and gifts whatever I decide. I can cancel or suspend my subscription at any time. I am over 18 years of age.

Name Mrs/Miss/Ms/Mr _____ EP17R

Address _____

_____

Postcode _____ Signature _____

Offer expires 31st May 1992. The right is reserved to refuse an application and change the terms of this offer. Readers overseas and in Eire please send for details. Southern Africa write to Book Services International Ltd, P.O. Box 41654, Craighall, Transvaal 2024. You may be mailed with offers from other reputable companies as a result of this application.

If you would prefer not to share in this opportunity, please tick box. ☐

Mills & Boon

Next month's Romances

Each month, you can chose from a world of variety in romance with Mills & Boon. These are the new titles to look out for next month.

ONCE BITTEN, TWICE SHY ROBYN DONALD
SAVING GRACE CAROLE MORTIMER
AN UNLIKELY ROMANCE BETTY NEELS
STORMY VOYAGE SALLY WENTWORTH
A TIME FOR LOVE AMANDA BROWNING
INTANGIBLE DREAM PATRICIA WILSON
IMAGES OF DESIRE ANNE BEAUMONT
OFFER ME A RAINBOW NATALIE FOX
TROUBLE SHOOTER DIANA HAMILTON
A ROMAN MARRIAGE STEPHANIE HOWARD
DANGEROUS COMPANY KAY GREGORY
DECEITFUL LOVER HELEN BROOKS
FOR LOVE OR POWER ROSALIE HENAGHAN
DISTANT SHADOWS ALISON YORK
FLORENTINE SPRING CHARLOTTE LAMB

STARSIGN
HUNTER'S HAREM ELEANOR REES

Available from Boots, Martins, John Menzies, W.H. Smith, most supermarkets and other paperback stockists.

Also available from Mills & Boon Reader Service, P.O. Box 236, Thornton Road, Croydon, Surrey CR9 3RU.